"You're Skye Henderson?"

Instead of looking suitably dazzled, the puzzlement in Lorimer's eyes deepened to what Skye recognized as suspicion.

"I have to admit that you're not exactly what I was expecting," he said at last.

"Aren't I?" she said a little nervously. "What were you expecting me to be like?"

"Let's say that I was expecting someone a little less...colorful."

Dear Reader,

It's raining men! Welcome to Harlequin Romance's new miniseries, **Holding Out for a Hero.** Every month for a whole year we'll be bringing you some of the world's most eligible men. They're handsome, they're charming but, best of all, they're single! And as twelve lucky women are about to discover it's not finding Mr. Right that's the problem—it's holding on to him!

This month it's the turn of award-winning author Jessica Hart with *The Right Kind of Man* (#3406). In the coming months look out for books with our **Holding Out for a Hero** flash by some of Harlequin Romance's best-loved authors: Leigh Michaels, Betty Neels, Lucy Gordon and Rebecca Winters. Next month it's the turn of Jeanne Allan with *Moving in With Adam.*

This is one series you don't want to miss!

With best wishes,

The Editors
Harlequin Romance

Some men are worth waiting for!

The Right Kind of Man
Jessica Hart

Harlequin Books

TORONTO • NEW YORK • LONDON
AMSTERDAM • PARIS • SYDNEY • HAMBURG
STOCKHOLM • ATHENS • TOKYO • MILAN
MADRID • WARSAW • BUDAPEST • AUCKLAND

For all at B. V.

ISBN 0-373-03406-7

THE RIGHT KIND OF MAN

First North American Publication 1996.

Copyright © 1994 by Jessica Hart.

This edition published by arrangement with Harlequin Books S.A.

® and TM are trademarks of the publisher. Trademarks indicated with
® are registered in the United States Patent and Trademark Office, the
Canadian Trade Marks Office and in other countries.

Printed in U.S.A.

CHAPTER ONE

'FRANKLY, Miss Henderson, you're quite unsuitable for the job.'

Skye looked at the man sitting behind the desk in dismay. Lorimer Kingan was one of those quiet, angular, unsmiling Scots with dark Celtic looks and an air of granite strength. What was it she had said to Vanessa? 'He'll be a pushover.' Her blue eyes dropped to the implacable line of his mouth and a peculiar sense of recognition shivered slowly down her spine. Lorimer Kingan might be many things, but a pushover was definitely not one of them. She had never met anyone less likely to be bowled over by her charm.

The interview had got off to a bad start. Lorimer had stood up as she was shown into his office, and his dark gaze had swept over her, from the wild golden curls to the contrasting jade strips across the toes of her turquoise suede shoes, in one comprehensive glance. Skye felt as if she had been examined, assessed and dismissed as a dizzy blonde before she had even opened her mouth.

It wasn't an entirely unjustified assessment, she was honest enough to admit to herself, but it was no part of her plan to tell Lorimer Kingan that. And anyway, she had changed. She was tired of being a dizzy blonde. Charles and her father were convinced that she was hopelessly scatty, but she was going to show them that she was perfectly capable of being sensible and surviving on her own. Unfortunately, to do *that* meant somehow persuading Lorimer that she was the epitome of a dedicated, efficient and professional PA. Reminded of her resolve, Skye had squared her shoulders and given him her best smile as he'd gestured her to the chair in front of his desk. Few men were proof against Skye's smile, but Lorimer was evidently made of sterner stuff. It had simply bounced off him, unnoticed, as he'd sat back behind his desk and picked up her c.v.

She had sat trying to look calm and composed as he reread her details, but his frown was making her nervous. Had he guessed just how wildly she had exaggerated? Vanessa had been appalled when she found Skye gaily typing out a shamelessly inaccurate c.v. on her word processor, but Skye had brushed aside her objections. 'It's only a few white lies,' she had said airily. 'Nobody ever checks a c.v.' Now she wasn't so sure. Lorimer Kingan looked like a man who would check *everything*.

After what seemed to Skye a very long time, he had put down the c.v. and looked at her. Somehow she felt that he should have had icy grey eyes to go with his air of cool implacability, but instead they were a deep, dark blue and made her think of wild water and brooding hills shrouded in mist. They were also uncomfortably acute.

He had glanced from her to the c.v. and then back again, evidently puzzled. '*You're* Skye Henderson?'

'Yes,' said Skye. She tried her smile again. At least he seemed to notice it this time, although the effect wasn't quite what she had anticipated. Instead of looking suitably dazzled, the puzzlement in his eyes deepened to curiosity then to what Skye recognised with a sinking feeling as suspicion.

'I have to admit that you're not exactly what I was expecting,' he said at last. His voice was dry with an irony that made it impossible to know exactly what he was thinking.

'Aren't I?' she said a little nervously. 'What were you expecting me to be like?'

'Let's say that I was expecting someone a little less...colourful.' The unsettling blue eyes rested on Skye, a vibrant figure in a short wool skirt and a baggy jumper that matched the brilliant colours on her shoes, and his expression of somewhat sardonic amusement deepened. He tapped her c.v. with his pen. 'Your career history is most impressive. I imagine that anyone who's held down the sort of jobs that you've had needs to be both discreet and efficient.' He studied her with a sort of impersonal speculation that made Skye shift uncomfortably in her chair. Curls the colour of silver gilt rioted uncontrollably about her vivid face with its dancing eyes and the wide, generous mouth that always seemed to be on the verge of curving into a smile, no matter how hard she tried to purse her lips into a serious expression. In spite of her efforts to look sensible, it appeared that Lorimer was unconvinced. 'You'll forgive me if I say that *discreet* isn't a word that immediately springs to mind when one looks at you. I must confess that I was expecting someone a little more professional in appearance,' he went on, and Skye couldn't decide whether he sounded amused or sarcastic. Either way, he wasn't impressed.

She met his eyes as confidently as she could. 'My last boss believed in judging people by their work, not by their appearance,' she said. 'After all, you don't type any quicker if you're wearing a grey suit.' It certainly didn't make any difference to her. She typed slowly no matter what she was wearing.

'Perhaps not,' Lorimer agreed with a glint of humour. Skye just hoped it wasn't at the thought of her in a grey

suit. 'However, I'm sure that someone with your qualifications and experience doesn't need me to tell you that
there's a lot more to being a secretary than typing.' Now
he was *definitely* being sarcastic! 'She also has to reflect
the image of the company. My clients are a conservative
lot, and I can't help feeling they might be wary of suddenly finding themselves dealing with a cross between a
rainbow and a one-woman carnival. We'd have to issue
sunglasses in Reception in case they were dazzled by the
sight of you!'

'You don't look very dazzled,' Skye pointed out rather
sourly. This interview would be a lot easier for her if he
were!

'Ah, but then I'm a particularly difficult man to impress!' Lorimer countered smoothly.

He could say that again! Skye suppressed a sigh, but
she wasn't ready to give up yet. 'I'll change,' she offered
generously. 'I'll wear brown tweed every day.'

The crease at the corner of his mouth deepened into
what was almost, but not quite, a smile. 'Far be it from
me to demand such a sacrifice!'

She hastened to reassure him. 'I wouldn't mind,
honestly. I'll be very quiet and wear whatever you want.
Your clients won't even notice me.'

Lorimer looked at her. She was leaning forward persuasively, long legs tucked under her chair, her face vivid.
Brightly coloured parrot earrings swung out through her
curls and brushed her cheeks.

'You're not the kind of girl who doesn't get noticed,'
he said, the undercurrent of sarcasm in his voice relaxing into reluctant amusement.

Skye didn't know whether to feel put out at his refusal
to take her seriously, or intrigued at the way the glimpse
of warmth altered his expression and hinted at a dis-

quietingly attractive man beneath the forbidding exterior. None of this was going to plan. Lorimer's letter inviting her to the interview had been so encouraging that she had been convinced that getting the job was a foregone conclusion. Vanessa had pointed out that any businessman worthy of the name would want some proof that his prospective secretary was everything that she had claimed, but Skye had pooh-poohed the idea, certain that all she would have to do was smile and look pretty. Now it looked as if Vanessa had been right.

Vanessa usually *was* right, Skye remembered belatedly. She only hoped that her friend wasn't right about Charles, too.

'Really, you won't even know I'm there,' she insisted with an edge of desperation, and Lorimer raised a derisive eyebrow.

'That's hardly a recommendation,' he said with some astringency. 'You're unlikely to prove a very effective assistant if I can't even tell whether you're in the office or not!'

Honestly, there was no pleasing him! 'A minute ago you said you didn't want anyone to notice me,' she pointed out sulkily.

Lorimer was beginning to lose patience. 'What I *want*,' he said bitingly, 'is an efficient, reliable secretary who understands the concept of moderation, not one who appears to think that the only alternative to overwhelming people is to go to the other extreme and fade away entirely!'

To Skye, it all sounded horribly familiar. Moderation, efficiency, reliability...why did men set so much store by them? Her father had spent years trying to din them into her, without any noticeable success, and even Charles seemed to find such dreary qualities irresistibly attractive. Skye couldn't understand it, but, if that was what he liked, that was how she would be. That was why she was here.

She set her chin doggedly. 'I *am* moderate,' she said. 'I'm extremely moderate.'

Lorimer sighed and picked up her c.v. once more. 'You seem very anxious to persuade me to give you the job, and yet I wouldn't have thought it was the obvious next step in your career plan. If you're as high-powered as you *claim* to be, surely you should be able to get a job anywhere?'

The sarcasm had crept back into his tone. Skye didn't like the way he had stressed 'claim', for all the world as if he didn't believe a word of her c.v.!

'Of course,' she said, trying to sound blasé. 'But I've decided to change direction and try something completely new.' That was true enough. A proper job was a new direction for her.

'I see.' Predictably enough, Lorimer was looking sceptical. 'I suppose you are aware that this is only a temporary job?'

'The advertisement said you wanted someone for three months,' said Skye, who had applied for that very reason. She might be determined to prove that she could hold down a proper job, but she didn't want to have to prove it for *too* long. Three months sounded about right.

'That's right,' said Lorimer. 'Catriona, who's been my secretary for four years now, has had to leave work earlier than she had planned. She's expecting a baby next year, but she's got high blood-pressure and the doctors have told her that she'll have to take things very easy for the next few months. Originally, we'd arranged that she would work up until Christmas, and Moira Lindsay would take over in January. That's still the plan. Moira is exceptionally well-qualified to do the job and I don't want to lose her, but she's committed to organising a big Pro-Am competition until December. Unfortunately, the next three months are going to be busy, so I need someone who's prepared to work hard, but there's no question of it turning into a permanent job.'

'That suits me.' Skye beamed at him hopefully. If Charles hadn't discovered that they were made for each other by Christmas, he never would. He *would*, though, Skye reminded herself fiercely. She had to think positive.

Lorimer's eyes were narrowed suspiciously. 'You say you want to change direction...why didn't you just find yourself a different job in London?'

'I wanted to make a completely fresh start,' said Skye grandly.

'So you came to Edinburgh?'

'Yes.'

'Why?'

'I've told you,' she said a little crossly. 'I wanted to make a complete break and start afresh somewhere new.'

'And I'm *asking* you why you chose Edinburgh,' said Lorimer through his teeth. 'What made you decide to come here, rather than Cardiff or Penzance or Manchester or any of the other places where you could have started afresh?'

Skye hesitated, wondering what he would say if she told him that the reason was six feet tall, devastatingly handsome and answered to the name of Charles. He was unlikely to be impressed.

Lorimer was waiting for her answer, his head bent as he made some neat notes on her c.v. Skye studied him with guileless blue eyes, glad of the opportunity to look at him without that hard stare boring into her. The angle of his head emphasised the severe planes of his face and the forceful nose. His mouth was stern. *Not* a sentimental type, she decided. He would never understand about Charles. In fact, she thought glumly, Lorimer Kingan didn't look like the kind of man who would have any time for love at all. Then she looked at his mouth again, remembering how reluctant amusement had tugged at one corner, and deep inside her doubt uncurled along with a strange, spreading warmth. He wouldn't love easily, but if he did . . .

'Well?' Lorimer's impatient voice broke into her thoughts and Skye was startled to find herself staring into his blue eyes. Her eyes were blue, too, but hers were the colour of an English summer sky dancing with sunshine, while his were deep and dark and, right now, distinctly unfriendly.

'Well?' she echoed blankly, so distracted by his mouth that she had completely forgotten his question.

'I asked why you chose to come to Edinburgh,' said Lorimer with exaggerated patience. 'Is it a state secret, or is it just that words of one syllable are too complicated for you to understand?'

Skye flushed at his acid tone. 'I—er—I wanted to get away from London for a while,' she improvised. Really, if she had known he was going to ask all these questions, she'd have done a bit more preparation.

'Why?' he said again.

'Personal reasons,' said Skye loftily, hoping that he would assume her reluctance to discuss the matter meant that it was something embarrassing and drop the subject, but the prospect of embarrassment evidently didn't bother Lorimer.

'Man trouble, I suppose?' he said, sitting back in his chair and surveying her critically.

Skye looked back at him warily. 'Why should you think that?'

'Because you look like the kind of girl I invariably associate with men or trouble, and usually both.'

If only she could fire up in righteous indignation! Skye contemplated denying the whole idea, but honesty forced her to accept that she probably wouldn't sound very convincing. The truth was, she *was* usually in trouble of some kind, and, yes, it was usually something to do with men too, though how Lorimer Kingan had guessed that she couldn't imagine.

Sometimes, her life seemed to be one long muddle... but all that was going to change now that she had met Charles, she reminded herself. He was the one who had made her realise how much her father spoilt her, and it was his preference for cool, capable women that had stung her into renouncing her previous happy, haphazard life. All she had to do was stay in Edinburgh so that he had a chance to realise how much she had changed, and how perfect they could be together.

If only she hadn't told him that she was working for Lorimer Kingan! Now she had landed herself in more trouble. She *had* to persuade Lorimer to give her the job. The alternative was too horrible to contemplate: telling Charles that she had lied, telling her father that she had failed, creeping back to London in disgrace. Always prone to dramatic exaggeration, Skye pictured herself pining away alone in some garret. The fact that all the garrets in her part of London had long been converted into top-floor flats, or that she had a large, adoring family and wide circle of affectionate friends, none of whom would allow her to pine, was conveniently forgotten. If she didn't get this job, she would die of a broken heart and it would all be Lorimer Kingan's fault!

Despair at this affecting and extremely unlikely scenario moved her to inspiration. 'I came to Edinburgh to be with a friend,' she said desperately, assuming a selfless expression. 'Her fiancé jilted her just before the wedding, and Vanessa's absolutely devastated.' This would be news to Vanessa who had never been engaged and was perfectly happy working for an up-market skiing company, but Skye was committed to her story now and crossed her fingers in her lap. 'I don't want her to be on her own too much, so I said I would come and stay with her for a couple of months until she was over the worst. That's why a temporary job would suit me so well,' she continued, blue eyes innocent. 'I don't want to commit myself to a permanent job, but I need to support myself while I'm with Vanessa. I can't let her down.'

Skye was rather pleased with this image of herself as a noble, supportive friend, but Lorimer was unmoved. 'I'm sure it's very admirable of you,' he said with the ironic inflexion which seemed so typical of him. Skye couldn't work out how it was that he kept his face utterly straight and yet managed to convey the impression that he found her utterly ridiculous. 'Moved as I am by your affecting story, I'm afraid I'm going to have to disappoint you and your unfortunate friend.'

'But why?' Skye's eyes were wide and blue with dismay at the finality in his voice. He must have a heart of stone. Either that, or he hadn't believed a word.

'Frankly, Miss Henderson, you're quite unsuitable for the job.' Lorimer pushed back his chair and got to his feet, prowling restlessly over to stand by the window looking out at the Georgian houses on the other side of the road. It was a bright, cold October day and the sun caught the elegant façades, making the polished-brass plates gleam and throwing shadows of the smartly painted wrought-iron railings against the pale stone.

'I asked you to come here today because of your impressive-looking c.v. and because I thought that with a name like Skye Henderson and an Edinburgh address you would be a Scot. I have to say that if I had known that you were English I wouldn't have invited you. You *are* English, aren't you?'

'Does it matter?' asked Skye cautiously.

'Yes, Miss Henderson, it does.'

'I'm half Scottish,' she offered, thinking quickly. In for a penny, in for a pound.

Lorimer turned. He looked at Skye and his mouth twitched. 'It's not a very obvious half,' he said, moving around the desk towards her. He looked very tall and unnervingly powerful with the light behind him and Skye felt at a distinct disadvantage sitting down. It had been easier when he was sitting behind the desk. In his conventional suit and tie, she had been able to think of him as a businessman, a rather formidable one, perhaps, but a man like many others. Now, as he loomed over her, she had a quite different impression of him. She sensed a wildness in him, a passion like a banked fire, as if he belonged to the hills and the sea. Skye had never met anyone like him before, and deep within her she felt a tug of instinctive response. They could hardly be more different, but in her own way she too was a free spirit, impulsive and imprudent, but ready always to seize whatever life had to offer.

For a long moment, blue eyes stared into blue, then he took her chin in his hand and forced her face up. 'Which half of you is Scottish, Skye Henderson?' he

asked softly. 'You don't look very Scottish to me.' Skye
was very aware of his fingers against her skin. They were
warm and strong and something about his touch set her
pulse booming and beating with a nervous excitement.
'No,' he went on, still looking down at her with narrowed eyes. She felt as if he could see right through her.
'I don't think you're a Scot. You're very pretty and very
frivolous and very English.'

'W-what does it matter?' said Skye a little breathlessly
as he released her and stepped back.

'I'll tell you.' Lorimer propped himself on the front
of his desk and folded his arms. The amusement that so
confused her had vanished from his eyes, leaving them
cool and shuttered. 'Do you know what we do here at
Kingan Associates?'

'Something to do with golf,' said Skye cautiously,
glancing at the series of stunning photographs on the
wall.

Lorimer followed the direction of her gaze. 'Very per-
ceptive of you,' he said, not bothering to disguise his
sarcasm this time, and clearly unimpressed by her lack
of research. 'To be more specific, we design and develop
new golf courses,' he said. 'Golf, like so many other
leisure activities, is a booming business nowadays.
Existing golf clubs are over-subscribed, and there's a
tremendous demand for new courses. At the same time,
farmers are being encouraged to produce less and to set
aside agricultural land for other purposes. That's where
we come in. Over the past few years, we've bought up
land that would otherwise be lying fallow and developed
a number of new courses around Scotland. They're wel-
comed by the tourist industry and local communities
alike, especially as we've made a point of providing more
opportunities for young people to learn, by sponsoring

competitions and providing additional holes and practice areas specifically for junior members.'

A little lost by all of this, Skye found herself thinking what a nice voice he had. Not a broad accent, but that distinctively Scottish intonation that was so easy on the ear. Warmer and softer than the English voices she was used to, it still had an undercurrent of steel that seemed to resonate deep inside her.

'I don't quite see what this has to do with my being English... half English,' she corrected herself quickly.

'Possibly not,' said Lorimer caustically. 'I'm trying to explain the background as all I've seen of you so far hasn't led me to have any great confidence in your ability to grasp the point I'm making without it!' He paused and watched Skye subside mutinously before he went on. 'Kingan Associates has been extremely successful and we're currently working on projects designing courses in Europe, Japan and America as well as here in the UK. However, now that we've proved ourselves on the golf front, I'm anxious to keep the company developing in new directions, and I'm trying to expand our operations into hotels offering the highest quality sporting facilities. I'm interested in a site in Galloway as a flagship complex, but for such an ambitious change of direction to succeed I've got to find additional capital to cover the initial development costs.'

Not daring to interrupt again, Skye watched in silence as Lorimer propped himself against his desk. 'All went well at first,' he went on. 'A financial company in London were interested and agreed to provide the necessary investment to get the project going, but when I was halfway through the negotiations to buy the

property they suddenly decided to send up one of their
female executives to "oversee" the arrangements.'

His voice hardened. 'I was prepared to accept an
overseer if it was a condition of the investment, but this
woman meddled in arrangements that simply didn't
concern her. She succeeded in putting everyone's back
up, mine most of all, and before I knew what had happened the owners of the properties involved had withdrawn from the deal altogether. That was the end of my
English association!' He picked up a bronze statue of a
golfer from his desk and turned it in his hands as if remembering his frustration. 'Had it been any other
project, I might have cut my losses, but the Galloway
hotel is important to me personally. It's a dream I've
had for some time now, and I know I can make it work.
I also know that I've found the perfect location, and
I'm not going to give it up.'

Putting down the statue, Lorimer glanced at Skye.
'I've managed to talk most of the different parties round
again,' he said, 'and I'm depending on raising the extra
capital from an Edinburgh company this time, but I'm
sure you'll understand that I can't afford to risk alienating everyone again by employing someone quite as
English as you.'

Skye shifted uneasily under his sardonic gaze, aware
for the first time of just how out of place she looked.
His office was a large, well-proportioned room, tra-
ditionally furnished in polished wood and leather. It was,
Skye thought, a very masculine room, soberly decorated, with no concessions to frivolity. In the middle of
it all, she sat like a butterfly, a vibrant splash of colour,
her earrings swinging jauntily, warm and gaudy and un-
deniably feminine.

It was a daunting situation, but Skye could be just as stubborn as Lorimer. He might be determined not to give up his location, but she was equally determined not to give up her one chance of impressing Charles.

'I don't see that it matters,' she objected. 'Nobody needs to know that it's an English girl typing your letters. Word processors don't have accents.'

'Word processors don't answer the phone or make appointments or greet visitors either,' Lorimer pointed out scathingly. 'A dumb assistant isn't much use to me.'

Skye wasn't beaten yet. 'I could always talk like this,' she suggested, putting on a typically Edinburgh accent. She was an excellent mimic and had been keeping Vanessa in fits with her imitations of her excruciatingly genteel neighbour, but Lorimer was not amused.

'You appear to think this is some kind of game,' he said, straightening. 'Or is the ability to talk in a silly accent just another of your much vaunted professional skills?' He sat down behind his desk once more and regarded Skye across its ordered expanse. 'No, I've already explained the situation. I'm staking my personal reputation on the success of the Galloway project, and I can't afford to risk employing the wrong kind of secretary. I need someone sensible and efficient, someone dedicated and discreet...and Scottish.' The deep blue eyes gleamed with sardonic amusement. 'You, Miss Henderson, don't seem to me to fit into any of those categories, no matter what your c.v. says.'

'That's not fair,' she protested. 'I can't help being English.'

'An unfortunate disadvantage of birth,' he agreed, 'but not one either of us can do much about. If it makes you feel any better, it's not just your nationality that's against you. As it said in the advertisement, I need an assistant who knows something about golf. Frankly, the ability to tell one end of a golf club from another is much more important to me than all your quite astonishing qualifications!'

Skye cast Lorimer a jaundiced look. She had spent *hours* inventing impressive degrees and secretarial skills for herself, but she might as well not have bothered for all the notice Lorimer seemed to take of them! She could have watched her favourite soap opera after all, she remembered, obscurely resentful.

'I didn't put it down because I don't have any formal qualifications,' she said with a tinge of desperation. 'But I really am terribly interested in golf.'

Lorimer quirked a disbelieving eyebrow. 'You don't look like a golfer.'

'I'm just a beginner,' she said hastily, praying that he wouldn't whisk her off to a golf course for a demonstration of her great interest.

'Have you got a handicap?'

Skye stared at him before she remembered the crash course in golf terminology that Vanessa had given her last night. It was something to do with penalising players…wasn't it? Anyway, all serious golfers had one. 'Oh, yes,' she said with breezy confidence. 'Of course.' Not knowing the first thing about it must count as a handicap if nothing else!

'A high one, I suppose?'

'No,' said Skye firmly, suspecting sarcasm. 'Very low.' There was no point in pretending to be too clever. 'My handicap's just two at the moment,' she went on, so that he got the message and didn't expect too much of her.

'Two?' Lorimer's expression was unreadable, and Skye wondered if she had miscalculated. Perhaps he was going to insist that he wanted a brilliant player?

'I'm hoping to improve while I'm in Scotland,' she assured him.

'I see.' For a moment Lorimer just looked at her and then, suddenly, unexpectedly, his mouth twitched into a devastating grin that took Skye quite unawares and drove the breath from her lungs with the force of a blow. She had sensed the amusement lurking intriguingly behind the austere, even dour lines of his face, but even so she was totally unprepared for the way the humour lit his expression and revealed a charm that was all the more striking for being so well-concealed. Who would have guessed that he could look so much younger, so much warmer, so dangerously attractive?

'You don't give up easily, do you?' he said, exasperation lacing the resigned amusement in his voice.

'Isn't that a good trait?' With difficulty, Skye got her breathing under control.

'In some cases, but in yours...' Lorimer shook his head. 'No, the combination of frivolity and stubbornness is too awful to contemplate!'

'Oh, please!' Skye threw pride to the wind and begged as she realised that the worst was going to happen. How was she going to tell Charles? 'I'll do anything! I'll work really hard and I'll try not to sound too English and I'll wear dreary clothes and only speak when I'm spoken to if only you'll give me the job!' Clutching her hands together, she leant beseechingly towards him, her eyes blue and pleading. 'Please!'

Lorimer studied her thoughtfully for a moment. 'I wish I knew just why you're so desperate to have this job.'

'I've told you, I——'

'Spare me!' he interrupted, glancing at his watch and getting to his feet. 'I can't cope with any more affecting stories about jilted fiancées or your tremendous interest in golf, and as I have another appointment now it looks as if I'll never know the real reason.' His eyes glinted down at her. 'A pity, as I'm sure it would have been most entertaining!'

He walked over to the door and waited with what Skye was sure was mock-courtesy for her to stand up reluctantly. Clutching her bag to her chest, she wondered if it would be worth throwing herself at his feet in a final appeal, but one glance at his face was enough to make her change her mind. The brief glimpse of humour had vanished, leaving his expression as implacable as before. Any such dramatic gesture would make him recoil in horror, she realised sadly. He reached for the door-handle, clearly impatient for her to leave.

With a sigh, Skye resigned herself to the inevitable. It was just her luck that Lorimer Kingan had turned out to be such a chilly soul, she thought glumly as she walked towards him, before her eyes dropped unthinkingly to his mouth and she remembered how he had smiled.

Not *that* chilly.

'Goodbye, Miss Henderson,' he said, holding out his hand with one of his disconcertingly ironic looks. 'I'm sure that someone with your...shall we say...*original* approach won't have any difficulty finding another employer more susceptible to your charms.'

'I don't want anyone else,' she said as she took his hand, too disconsolate to think about what she was saying. 'I want you.'

'I'm immensely flattered, of course, but I'm afraid even the promise of such devotion isn't enough to make me change my mind!'

His fingers closed firmly around hers, and, appalled, Skye heard her words again as if in an echo. 'I want you'. Scarlet colour surged into her cheeks and she snatched her hand away.

'I didn't mean . . . I meant . . .' she stammered, horribly conscious of the way her skin was tingling where their hands had touched.

'I know what you meant,' said Lorimer drily, and opened the door.

Still blushing furiously, Skye walked past him into the reception area. Struggling to master her confusion, she didn't at first notice the man waiting in one of the comfortable armchairs, but as she and Lorimer appeared he put aside his newspaper and rose to his feet, a solidly built man in his fifties with iron-grey hair and shrewd eyes.

'Skye?'

Skye stopped dead in her tracks, unconscious of Lorimer's sudden tension. 'Fleming!' she cried in astonished delight as she recognised one of her father's oldest friends. Like her father, he was an astute financier who divided his time between his companies in London and Edinburgh. Skye had known him for as long as she could remember, but always thought of him in the context of her parents and home. It seemed strange to see him here in Edinburgh, but it made his familiar face all the more welcome and she threw herself into his arms and hugged him with typically exuberant abandon. 'What a wonderful surprise! What are you doing here?'

'I've come to see Lorimer here,' Fleming explained, returning her hug affectionately. 'We're working on an exciting deal together.' He released Skye and turned to Lorimer with a pleasant smile. 'Good to see you again, Lorimer.'

The two men shook hands. Lorimer's expression was wooden and Skye glanced from one to the other and belatedly put two and two together. Of course! Charles had implied that he had some dealings with Kingan Associates, and Charles worked for Fleming. Why hadn't it clicked before? *Fleming* was the investor Lorimer was so anxious not to offend.

'Charles told me that you were working here,' Fleming said to Skye, oblivious to the tension between her and Lorimer. 'I gather he bumped into you the other day? I must say I was surprised, but absolutely delighted to hear it! Does your father know?'

Skye didn't dare look at Lorimer. 'Er, not yet,' she said.

'He'll be very thankful to know that you've ended up in such good hands,' said Fleming jovially. He knew more than most people how Sky's adoring but exasperated father despaired over his daughter's erratic career. 'I've a good mind to ring him and tell him myself. Of course, I've always told him that there was no need to worry about you. "Skye's not nearly as scatty as she looks", I said to him, and Lorimer obviously agrees with me.' He beamed at Lorimer who was looking very grim. 'This is quite a coincidence! I've known Skye since she was a baby and I didn't think she ever went further north than the M25 in all that time, but suddenly she turns up in Edinburgh and working for you!'

'Quite a coincidence,' said Lorimer through set teeth. Skye stole a glance at him under her lashes. A muscle was beating furiously in his jaw. He looked like a man who could feel himself being forced into a corner and she bit her lip, wondering if she should tell Fleming that nothing was agreed. But that would mean Charles would know too... Lorimer could explain the true situation, she reasoned, even though Fleming's obvious delight at her supposed job had put him in an impossible situation. Would he risk alienating him by telling Fleming exactly what he thought of his friend's daughter?

'Well, time is money, so we'd better get on with our discussions,' said Fleming, suddenly businesslike. He kissed Skye on the cheek. 'Marjorie's up as well, so you must come and have dinner. We'll ask Charles too. I seem to remember you were rather struck by him at that party!'

'That would be lovely,' said Skye weakly.

Lorimer looked at his watch and then at his office. 'I'll be with you in a moment,' he said pointedly to Fleming, who took the hint and strolled towards the office with a final wave to Skye.

Skye was left looking nervously up into Lorimer's grim face. 'Did you know Fleming Carmichael was a potential investor in my project?' he asked tightly.

'No,' she said. 'I suppose if I'd thought about it I could have worked it out from something someone said to me, but it simply never occurred to me that I'd meet him here.' She hesitated. 'Are you going to tell him that I'm not working for you after all?'

'How can I, now?' Lorimer ran a hand through his hair in a gesture of exasperation. 'I don't know him well enough to know how he'd react. I've had enough complications setting up this deal as it is, without provoking yet another party into pulling out! If the prospect of seeing you here makes a difference to Fleming, well, it'll probably make it worth putting up with you after all.'

Skye let out a long breath of relief. 'You won't regret it,' she promised him.

'You'd better make sure I don't,' he said, and strode off towards his office.

'When do you want me to start?' she called after him.

Lorimer stopped and looked over his shoulder to where she stood uncertainly, still trying to grasp her luck in meeting Fleming just then. Across the hall, his blue eyes were dark and hostile. 'I won't make the obvious answer to that,' he said bitingly. 'Just be here on Monday morning, nine o'clock sharp.' Turning, he reached for the door-handle. 'And don't be late!'

CHAPTER TWO

VANESSA lived on the fourth floor of a typically gaunt and grey Edinburgh tenement building. Inside, the flats were spacious and high-ceilinged, but Skye dreaded the long plod up the worn stairs. At least it kept her fit, she thought, letting the heavy front door slam to behind her and peering up to where the skylight permitted a miserly amount of light to penetrate the dim stairwell.

Taking a deep breath, Skye set off up the first flight at a run to gain momentum. She lost it halfway up the second when she came across Vanessa's neighbour, Mrs Forsyth, struggling with two heavy bags of shopping. Mrs Forsyth always wore a coat and gloves and a felt turban-like hat secured at the front with an uncompromising button. Skye was convinced that she wore this outfit the whole time, even in bed. For her part, Mrs Forsyth thoroughly disapproved of Skye who was too pretty and, in her opinion, flighty. She pursed her lips and looked sour when she saw her now, but Skye only smiled sunnily back at her.

'Let me help you with those bags, Mrs Forsyth.'

Together, they laboured up the stairs, Skye chatting gaily in between puffs and Mrs Forsyth unbending enough to thank her when they reached the top at last. Skye felt as if she'd been given the George Cross.

'This is my day!' she cried as she burst into Vanessa's flat to find her friend drinking tea in the kitchen. 'Not only did I get the job, but Mrs Forsyth acknowledged my existence!'

'You got the job?' Vanessa put down her mug and stared at Skye in amazement. 'How on earth did you manage that?'

'I don't know why you have to sound so surprised.' Skye grinned and poured herself a mug of tea. 'Why shouldn't I get it?'

'I've been asking around about Lorimer Kingan at work, and it turns out that he's got quite a reputation.'

Skye pulled out a chair and sat down on the other side of the table. 'Oh?'

'There seems to be a lot of admiration and respect for him in the sports world. The courses that he's developed are supposed to be fantastic and they say he's done wonderful work with young players. Apparently he built that company out of nothing...I thought he sounded rather formidable.'

A vision of Lorimer rose before Skye: the dark blue eyes, the tough, forbidding lines of his face, the sense of massive strength. 'He was formidable all right,' she said. She could still feel the pressure of his palm against hers, the tingling warmth of his skin.

'He can't have been that tough if he gave you the job,' Vanessa pointed out. 'Surely he didn't fall for that ridiculous c.v. you made up?'

'I don't think so.' Skye sounded regretful. 'Actually, I got the impression he didn't believe a word I said.'

'Then why did he give you the job?'

'Well...' Skye took a sip of her tea and told Vanessa all about the interview and the surprise meeting with Fleming. 'Lorimer wasn't very pleased,' she finished, 'but I can't help thinking that Fleming's appearing like that means that fate meant me to have the job!'

Vanessa looked dubious. 'If I were Lorimer Kingan, I'd be a lot more than "not very pleased"—I'd be furious with you for putting me in a situation like that!'

'Pooh!' Skye had recovered her usual breezy optimism once away from Lorimer's sharp eyes. 'He wanted a secretary and he's got one. I might not have been his first choice,' she allowed generously, 'but I'm free to start work when he wants and I'll do the job just as well as any other temp.'

'That'll be the day!' Vanessa grinned at her friend with affectionate scepticism. 'You don't know the first thing about golf, you're hopeless at typing, you could illuminate a medieval manuscript in the time it takes you to write a line of shorthand. The whole idea of efficiency is completely alien to you. You're muddled and irresponsible and you'll spend your whole time talking. Not to put too fine a point on it, Skye, I should think you'll drive Lorimer Kingan round the bend!'

'But I'm really going to try this time!' Skye protested. 'I'll make a success of this job, just you wait and see.'

'You never have before!'

'It's different now. You know, Van,' she went on seriously, 'until I met Charles I didn't realise how spoilt I was. I just had a good time and if things went wrong I knew my father would rescue me. It was Charles who made me see that I had to stand on my own two feet. He likes women who are cool and elegant and capable of looking after themselves. That's why I could never get him to take me seriously. As far as he was concerned, I was just a daddy's girl. It was awful when I realised that he didn't want anything to do with me, but looking back I think it was the best thing that could have happened. It made me take stock of my life,' she concluded grandly, and looked affronted when Vanessa only grinned. 'It's true,' she insisted. 'I realised that if I wanted to have any chance with Charles I would have to change my life completely. I feel guilty whenever I think about all the times I've let Dad bail me out. I should have left London and learnt to be independent long ago. This is my chance to prove to him as well as to Charles that I can survive by myself.'

'Can you?' asked Vanessa with a quizzical look.

'I can try,' said Skye, who had a much stronger, more stubborn will than most people gave her credit for. 'Coming to Edinburgh was just what I needed to make a fresh start. Poor Dad's been desperate for me to settle down and get myself a decent job, and now I'm going to make him proud of me for a change. *And* I'm going to show Charles that he can't get rid of me that easily. I'm going to be just as practical and professional as his other girlfriends. He'll never be interested in me as long as he just sees me as some scatty blonde.'

'But Skye, you *are* a scatty blonde! Wouldn't you like a man to love you for being the way you are?'

Skye hunched her shoulders, cradling the mug between her hands. 'It's so boring when they just sit and adore you,' she said glumly. 'I'm tired of boyfriends turning themselves into doormats. At least Charles doesn't do that.'

'That's because he's only interested in himself,' said Vanessa astringently. She had met Charles on a couple of occasions when she had been to stay with Skye in London and she had not been impressed. 'You only think you're in love with him because he's a challenge, but he's not the man for you, Skye, honestly he isn't. He's too cold. He wants his girlfriends to fit in with his image as some cool, ruthless, City type, and you'll never do that.'

'Yes, I will.' Skye looked stubborn. 'And I *am* in love with him. I wouldn't have come all the way up to Edinburgh and gone to all that trouble to get the job if I weren't, would I?'

'There's no telling what you'd do once you get an idea into your head,' said Vanessa with brutal honesty. 'The trouble with you, Skye, is that you do everything by extremes. You never just like a man, you lose your head completely. You fall in and out of love—or what you think is love—like a Yo-Yo, and it's always with the wrong kind of man. What you need is to fall *really* in love.'

Unbidden, Lorimer's image flickered in Skye's mind before she pushed it firmly away. She was in love with Charles; of course she was. Closing her eyes, she tried to conjure up Charles in her imagination, but all she could see was Lorimer's austere face with its ironic eyes and the stern, unexpectedly exciting mouth that had relaxed into that brief, tantalising tug of amusement.

Her eyes snapped open and she frowned. She didn't want to think about Lorimer. She wanted to think about Charles with his... In a sudden excess of panic, she realised that she couldn't picture him at all. She knew he was handsome, really *much* better-looking than Lorimer. It was just that all the details of his appearance seemed to have faded from her mind.

What did it matter, anyway? The important thing was that she loved him. She had already decided to play it cool so that Charles would never guess that he was the only reason for her appearance in Edinburgh, and now she had the perfect excuse for meeting him. He would come into the office and instead of the madcap girl he had known in London he would see her as Lorimer's discreetly efficient PA, cool, sophisticated, dedicated to

her job. He would be *bound* to fall in love with her then,
Skye reassured herself. And in the meantime she would
show Lorimer Kingan that she wasn't quite as silly as he
so obviously thought her. She would be the best secretary he had ever had and impress him so much with
her calm competence that he would quite forget that she
was English at all.

Convinced by this rosy picture of the next three
months, Skye stretched her arms contentedly above her
head and gave Vanessa a seraphic smile. 'Don't worry,
Van, everything's going to work out perfectly, I can feel
it in my bones. Love is on its way.'

On Monday morning, Skye set off in high spirits. It was
an early October day and the air held a distinctly autum-
nal bite, but the sky was a crisp, clear blue. Walking
down to wait for a bus opposite The Meadows, she
looked across at the trees, blazing gold and copper and
bronze, and told herself that by the time the leaves had
fallen her life would have changed completely. Skye
hugged herself at the thought.

'It's not warm, is it?' said the woman standing beside
her in the bus queue, and before long they were deep in
conversation, passing easily from the weather to the
problems of winter, her neighbour's arthritis, her grandchildren and what the doctor had said about young
Jimmy's tonsils. Always friendly to a fault, Skye listened,
absorbed, nodding sympathetically every now and then,
quite oblivious to the other passengers shuffling and
muttering and glancing irritably at their watches. It was
only when her new-found friend remarked on how late
the bus was that Skye thought to look at the time.

A quarter to nine! Lorimer's parting words rang om-
inously in her ears: 'And don't be late'. She would never

get down to the office in time, even if the bus came. Skye gulped and looked frantically up and down the road for a taxi, but the traffic was practically at a standstill. She was just going to have to run.

Kingan Associates was an imposing Georgian building in Edinburgh's famous New Town. By the time Skye clutched at its railings for support as she gasped for breath, she was exhausted, pale blonde hair hanging in a wild tangle around her scarlet face. She had never run so far or so fast in her life. Her breath was coming in great whoops, but somehow she forced herself upright and up the steps to the glossily painted white door with its gleaming brass and elegant fanlight.

Pushing open the door, Skye stepped cautiously into the hall, relieved to see that it was empty except for Sheila, the shy receptionist who had shown her into Lorimer's office for the interview. She looked at Skye's red face in some alarm.

'Are you all right?'

'No bus,' Skye croaked, wheezing and mopping at her face. So much for impressing Lorimer's office with her calmness and competence!

Sheila opened her mouth, but before she had a chance to reply the door to Lorimer's office opened with a snap.

'You're late.'

Skye's heart, already pounding with effort, seemed to stop altogether as she saw Lorimer standing in the doorway, with his fierce blue glare and his brows drawn over his nose in a forbidding line. He looked tougher, grimmer, altogether more disturbing than she remembered.

'I'm sorry,' she began, blaming her frantic run for the uncomfortable lurch of her heart and the breathless feeling at the back of her throat. 'The——'

'Come in here,' he barked, cutting her off before she had a chance to explain. 'I'm not going to talk to you where the whole office can hear.' Turning abruptly, he disappeared back into his room.

Sheila cast her a sympathetic glance but Skye only grimaced at his back and followed him reluctantly.

'Shut the door,' he ordered as she hesitated on the threshold, and then pointed at a chair. 'Sit down.'

'Yes, sir,' Skye muttered under her breath, wondering if he expected her to goose-step across the room. Deciding not to antagonise him any further, she sat gingerly on the edge of the chair and blew the curls off her forehead. The clip she had used to keep the hair out of her eyes so neatly that morning had come adrift as she'd run down the Lothian Road and now the silver gilt mass tumbled wildly about her face. She was acutely conscious of her crimson cheeks and dishevelled appearance, and had a nasty feeling that there was a huge ladder running all the way up the back of her new pair of tights. She glanced down, twisting her leg round surreptitiously. There was.

Lorimer was watching her with distaste, but as he took in the full extent of her disastrous appearance the grimness that had been in his eyes faded to an exasperation tinged with more than a hint of reluctant amusement. 'Do you possess a watch?' he asked with deceptive mildness.

'Yes,' said Skye, surprised but relieved that he didn't seem nearly as angry as he had at first. Snapping her heels together to hide the run, she sat up straighter and tried to look eager rather than exhausted.

'Do you know how to tell the time with it?' Lorimer persevered in the same tone of exaggerated patience.

'Yes, it's digital,' she explained kindly.

He closed his eyes briefly. 'No doubt that helps! Now, since you have a watch and we've established that you're able to read it, perhaps you could tell me what the time is?'

Even Skye couldn't mistake the heavy irony. She pulled back her sleeve and peered at her watch. 'Um...nine twenty-seven.'

'And what time were you supposed to be here?'

'Nine o'clock,' she said in a small voice.

'Nine o'clock,' he agreed. 'That makes you...?'

'Twenty-seven minutes late,' said Skye, feeling about two inches high.

Lorimer sat back in his chair. 'Marvellous! You can count as well as tell the time!'

'I would have been on time, but the bus was late,' she tried to explain.

'It didn't occur to you to look at your watch, which we now know you can read so cleverly, and make alternative arrangements once you knew the bus wasn't going to be on time?'

Skye eyed him warily, unsure of how to deal with his sarcasm. 'I didn't think about it,' she admitted, opting for the truth. 'You see, this woman was telling me about her grandson. You wouldn't believe the trouble they've had with his tonsils...'

She trailed off as she caught Lorimer's eye. 'I'm not interested in tonsils,' he said, speaking very carefully as if he was only keeping his temper in check with great difficulty. 'Everyone else in this office manages to get to work on time, and I'm not making any exceptions for you. I don't care how fascinating your conversations are; you'll be here at nine o'clock on the dot every morning, or you're out on your ear. Is that understood?'

Deciding it was safer to say nothing, Skye nodded.

'You know as well as I do that if it hadn't been for Fleming Carmichael you wouldn't be sitting there now,' he went on coldly. 'You're the last person I'd have chosen as my secretary, but Fleming seemed enthusiastic about the idea of you working here and frankly I'm prepared to do anything to keep him on my side at the moment. My priority is getting the investment so that I can get things moving on the new project, even if it means putting up with *you* for the next three months.'

'Thanks for the warm welcome!' said Skye huffily.

'I'm being honest,' he pointed out. 'And since we're on the subject of honesty, isn't it time you were honest with me?'

'Honest?' she echoed cautiously, and Lorimer sighed.

'I did wonder whether you'd recognise the word! How can I put it more simply...? We've discovered that you do, in fact, know how to tell the time, in spite of all evidence to the contrary. Now I want to know whether, if pushed to it, you can tell the truth.'

Skye's heart sank. 'What do you mean?' she said, but without very much conviction. She had a nasty feeling that she knew exactly what he meant.

Leaning forward over his desk, Lorimer fixed her with a keen blue stare. 'I had an interesting little chat with Fleming after you'd gone. He's obviously very fond of you.' Lorimer's tone made it clear that he found it hard to understand why. 'It never occurred to him that you wouldn't have been entirely honest with me, so I was able to find out quite a bit about you. Reading between the lines, I gather you've been spoilt and indulged all your life with the result that you're now irredeemably frivolous and irresponsible, as well as quite incapable of sticking at a job for more than a few months at a time.' He sat back in his chair without taking his eyes off Skye's face. 'Oh, don't worry, Fleming didn't say that. He seems to think that you've got enough charm and personality to survive anywhere, but I'm afraid I don't see it like that.' His voice changed. 'As I see it, you've lied to me, and I don't like liars.'

Skye burned with humiliation but her face was already so red that Lorimer probably didn't notice her guilty flush. 'I wanted the job, you see,' she explained in a small voice.

'I'd already gathered that from the interview,' said Lorimer, still scathing. 'Would you mind telling me exactly *why* I'm to have you inflicted on me? And this time I'd appreciate the truth!'

She swallowed. 'You'll think I'm stupid.'

'I wouldn't be at all surprised!' he said with one of his sudden gleams of amusement that so unnerved her. 'Come on, out with it! This isn't the sort of job to interest someone like you. Why have you picked on me?'

'Are you sure you want the truth?' Skye asked, eyeing him doubtfully. 'You won't like it.'

'I don't like anything about this situation!'

'Well...' Skye took a deep breath and began. 'Fleming and his wife, Marjorie, had a party a few months ago and I met someone there...a man.'

Lorimer tapped his pen up and down impatiently. 'I don't want your life history, Skye. I just want to know why you're here now.'

'I'm telling you!' Skye's blue eyes were indignant. She picked up the threads of her story. 'I met Charles at Fleming's and I...well, I fell for him rather heavily. He was so different from anyone else I knew.' She paused, fiddling with one of her rings, as she remembered the party and Charles, so cool and remote. 'I saw him a few times after that, at dinner parties and things, but we never had a chance to...to get to know each other properly. Charles works for Fleming,' she went on after a moment. 'It turned out that he'd just heard that he was being sent up to the Edinburgh office, so naturally he didn't want to get involved with anyone at that stage, knowing that he would be leaving soon.'

'Go on,' said Lorimer in a voice of grim long-suffering. 'Do I gather that when he came up to Edinburgh you decided to come too?'

She nodded. 'I was at a bit of a loose end then.' No need to tell him that yet another firm had reluctantly decided that her warmth and friendliness simply weren't worth the muddle she left in her wake. Her father's disappointment had been the final impetus to her resolution to make a fresh start. 'I happened to be talking to an old schoolfriend who lives here and she said she had a spare room in her flat. She suggested that I come up here, and it seemed like the perfect opportunity. I'm a great believer in fate,' she added, trying to make Lorimer understand. 'Charles was in Edinburgh, suddenly there was Vanessa offering me a room here, I didn't have any ties in London...it just seemed *meant*.'

'Did it indeed?'

Skye ignored the sardonic note in his voice. 'Yes. You see, I thought that if I were up here at the same time as Charles he'd be less preoccupied than when he was in London and we'd have a better chance to get to know each other.'

She had also thought that all the glamorous women who always seemed to be hanging around Charles would be safely four hundred miles away in London, but she didn't tell Lorimer *that* either.

'So you followed him up here?' Lorimer sounded as if he couldn't quite believe what he was hearing. 'Did this unfortunate man know he was being pursued so relentlessly?'

'Of course not.' Having got into the swing of her story, Skye was beginning to relax. She leant forward confidentially. 'Men hate that, don't they?'

'I can't imagine anything worse,' said Lorimer distantly, eyeing her with appalled fascination.

'Exactly! So I thought I'd have to make my presence here look natural, but I didn't really want to get involved in a permanent job in case it didn't work out with Charles. I decided I'd pretend I was up here doing a temporary job. I wasn't actually going to *do* the job, you understand. I was just going to tell Charles that was what I was doing up here and then get a job as a waitress or something to earn some money.'

Lorimer was looking resigned. 'It sounds a perverted sense of logic to me! Am I particularly stupid, or was there some reason you couldn't simply tell him that you were working as a waitress?'

Skye hesitated. 'Charles is very... serious, I suppose you'd call him.' Vanessa called him a snob, but then Vanessa had never liked him. 'He likes clever, professional girls. You know, the ones who wear smart suits and always know how to behave.' She sighed. For a moment, she had forgotten whom she was talking to, and it was a few moments before her dreamy eyes focused suddenly on Lorimer's. They held a very strange expression, exasperated and impatient, but there was a smile there too, and it was not an unkind one. If anything it was teasing, even tender, oddly disturbing, but the next instant it had vanished into a more familiar irony, jerking her back to the present.

'Do I understand that you're not exactly his type?' Lorimer asked drily.

'No,' she admitted sadly. 'Not exactly. I wanted to impress him, so I had to pretend to be doing something a little smarter than working in a restaurant. I looked in *The Scotsman* and saw your advertisement. It sounded ideal. Just three months, based here but some travelling around Scotland so I'd be able to say I was away when in fact I was at the restaurant.'

At the time, her plan had seemed perfect. Things had only begun to go wrong when she had met Charles again.

'So it was just my bad luck that you picked on my advertisement?' Lorimer asked with a sigh.

'Well, yes,' said Skye apologetically. 'I never thought I'd actually have to have anything to do with you. Everything was going so well. I managed to just "bump into" Charles and pretended to be terribly surprised to see him, and when he asked me what I was doing here I had my story all ready. I told him that I was working here, never dreaming that Kingan Associates would mean anything to him, but then he said he would probably see me at work, because he was involved in some deal with you. So then, of course, I had to get the job!'

Lorimer looked across at Skye without speaking. In honour of the new job, she had put on her least outrageous outfit, a short woollen dress in a vibrant cerise colour that clung to her slender figure and emphasised her long legs, but had been unable to resist jazzing up what she considered to be an unaccustomedly sober image by adding one of her collection of fun necklaces. This one was a string of exotic wooden fruits, all brightly painted. Wooden pineapples swung from her ears. She had finally succeeded in pushing the wild blonde curls away from her face and her blue eyes looked guilelessly back at him, certain that he would see the reasonableness of her argument.

'I don't suppose it occurred to you that there *were* alternatives?' he said after a moment. Skye had the impression that he had had to count to ten before he could allow himself to speak. 'You couldn't have told him you were still waiting to hear about the job? Or that you were still considering another offer? In fact, anything other than gaily claiming that you were already established as my PA?'

'I didn't think of it,' said Skye frankly. 'Anyway, the more I thought about it, the better idea it seemed. I can do just as good a job as anyone else, I just need the chance to prove it. If Charles came here, I'd have a good excuse to see him, and he'd be impressed to see me working as your PA. It would be a new image for me, you see: discreet, professional, sophisticated.'

Lorimer looked at the pineapples and winced visibly. 'If I thought there were any chance at all of you being any of those things, I wouldn't object to having you as my PA,' he said. 'As it is, I've never heard such a load of ridiculous nonsense in all my life!'

'You said you wanted the truth,' Skye reminded him a little sulkily. 'Don't you believe me?'

'Oh, I believe you all right! No one could make up an absurd story like that!' With a sigh, Lorimer put his head in his hands. 'What have I done to deserve this?'

Skye looked innocent. 'Perhaps you were very naughty once when you were a little boy?' she suggested helpfully, and then wished she hadn't when Lorimer lifted his head and glared at her. It was strange how eyes so blue and dark could look so icy, she thought irrelevantly.

'It isn't funny,' he said through clenched teeth. 'I'm trying to run a company here. I wanted a quiet, sensible assistant who would help me get the new project off the ground, and what do I get? A flippant featherbrain who's

as quiet as a Caribbean carnival and about as sensible!
You may find it an amusing situation, but I'm afraid I
don't. If this Charles of yours knows as much about you
as I do, I don't blame him for not wanting anything to
do with you. I never thought I'd feel any sympathy for
Charles Ferrars, but it seems I was wrong . . . I presume
we *are* talking about Charles Ferrars?'

She nodded and his eyes hardened. 'I've met him.
Fleming's anxious for him to get involved on this deal,
so it's possible he may be coming in, but if you want
him to see you as discreet, Skye, you'd better learn to
be discreet. You'll be dealing with confidential matters
that are none of Charles Ferrars' damned business, and
if I hear you talking to him about any of it, in or out
of office time, you'll be out with a well-deserved boot
up your backside. Is that clear?'

Skye sat up straighter. 'You mean you'll still let me
work for you?'

'It looks as if we're stuck with each other,' said
Lorimer, resigned. 'I don't want to risk offending
Fleming Carmichael, and you don't want your precious
Charles to know that you're here under entirely false
pretences, so now that we both know where we are we'd
better make the best of it. I would, however, like to know
exactly who, or what, I'm going to be dealing with for
the next three months!' Retrieving her c.v. from a pile
of papers on his desk, he tossed it contemptuously across
to her. 'Would it be fair for me to assume that this is a
tissue of lies from start to finish?'

Skye retrieved the c.v. and smoothed it over her knee.
'My name and address are right,' she began cautiously,
reading down the list of personal details. 'And I really
am twenty-three and single.'

'Good of you to be so candid,' he said with more than a touch of acid. 'Does this catalogue of true facts about Skye Henderson extend any further, or was four lines about as much as you could manage?'

She considered the list again. 'I was born in London...that's right too.'

'Hardly a recommendation, even if it is true,' said Lorimer. 'However, let's stick with your antecedents. Am I right in thinking that your mother is not in fact Scottish, as you claimed?'

'No...but she did go through a stage of being very keen on Scotland,' Skye offered helpfully. 'She goes through fads. At the moment, she's being very "green", but I don't suppose it'll last. Anyway, I think she was reading about Bonnie Prince Charlie just before I was born and got a bit carried away with the romance of it all. She's as English as you can get, but apparently she went around in a tartan skirt for a while and carried on as if my father were personally responsible for Culloden. I suspect he let her call me Skye just to shut her up for a while!' She laughed merrily, but Lorimer was not amused.

'Very funny,' he said coldly. 'That sort of flippant attitude is typical of the English, of course. They treat Scotland as if it's some kind of joke.' His tone was so bitter that Skye had the impression that his dislike of the English went back way beyond his disastrous involvement with the London finance company, and she looked at him curiously, wondering about his past and what had made him the man he was now.

Wisely deciding not to make matters any worse than they were already, she sat up straighter in her chair and tried to look like the kind of girl who didn't even know the meaning of the word 'joke', but her face simply wasn't designed to do anything other than smile.

Watching her unsuccessful attempts to appear suitably earnest, Lorimer's forbidding expression eased. He frowned harder and tried to look severe, but there was an unwilling but unmistakable gleam of humour in his eyes. He nodded at the c.v. in her lap. 'I gathered from what Fleming said that you've taken a...how shall I put it?...a somewhat *creative* approach as far as work experience is concerned?'

'I just promoted myself a bit,' said Skye, glancing guiltily at the list of high-powered jobs she had claimed for herself. Perhaps she *had* been rather ambitious.

'So you have worked for an advertising agency, but not as the managing director's PA?'

'I was a temp there for a couple of weeks.'

'A couple of weeks?' Lorimer pressed his fingers to his temples and breathed deeply. 'You don't lack nerve, I'll give you that! I suppose I should be grateful that you've worked as a secretary at all. At least it means you can type...or does it?'

'Of course I can!'

'At seventy words a minute?'

'Well, perhaps not quite that fast...'

'I didn't think it would be. How many words a minute should I deduct to give me a fair idea of what you can actually do? Twenty? Twenty-five?'

'Forty?' Skye hazarded a guess.

Lorimer kept his temper with a palpable effort. 'Forty?' he repeated, his voice carefully expressionless. 'Let me get this right. You can manage a bit of laborious typing, but I might as well learn to write all my letters out by hand rather than expect you to take down any shorthand?'

'I think it might be better,' said Skye, relieved.

'Is there anything you *can* do?'

'I can answer the phone,' she said brightly, but Lorimer only lifted a sardonic eyebrow.

'I hope you're not expecting a round of applause?'

'And I make a very good cup of coffee.'

'I'm sure that'll be a great help, but I'm more than capable of pouring my own coffee!'

Skye thought. 'Well...I can do the filing and the photocopying and make travel arrangements...and I could organise your social life.' She looked at him hopefully. She had always thought she would make rather a good social secretary, but somehow Lorimer didn't look the type to go in for long lunches or taking guests to the theatre. His idea of entertainment was probably a round of golf, she realised. Not much scope for her *there*.

Lorimer was unimpressed by her array of talents. 'If you type as slowly as it sounds, I'll be here all night waiting to sign my letters and I won't have time for a social life,' he pointed out caustically. 'Well, we seem to have established that your c.v. isn't worth the paper it's written on, so I might as well have it back.' He held out his hand and Skye gave it back to him rather shamefacedly. 'I was going to tear it up, but it's such a creative document that I think I'll keep it to remind me just how far some girls will go to get their man! I'm surprised you didn't list Charles Ferrars as one of your interests instead of...what was it now?...oh, yes, travel, theatre and, yes, golf!'

'I would like to play,' said Skye bravely, meeting his derisive look.

'But you've never been near a golf course in your life?'

'Well...no.'

'That was obvious,' said Lorimer. 'Even if it hadn't been plain as a pikestaff that you were making everything up as you went along, I'd have known you were bluffing as soon as you told me your handicap was two.'

'But I deliberately chose a low handicap so that you wouldn't suspect!'

Lorimer sighed. 'Ladies' handicaps begin at thirty-six, Skye. The better you are, the lower your handicap. If you play off two, you're an extremely good player. If you'd claimed a handicap in the thirties, I might just have believed that you'd recognise a golf ball if it fell on your head.'

'Well, what a stupid system!' said Skye, disgusted, and then giggled as she realised what a fool she had made of herself. 'It's just as well you didn't offer me a game!'

'I'm glad you find it so amusing,' said Lorimer dourly. 'We won't be able to make a scratch player out of you, but you're going to have to learn something about golf if you're not going to make me look utterly ridiculous.'

'Couldn't I pretend to have broken my arm or something?'

'Don't be ridiculous,' he said irritably. 'You can't spend three months in plaster for no reason. Besides, you need to sound as if you know what you're talking about on the phone. I'll have to show you the basics when we go down to Galloway. It's quiet down there and no one will see us.'

Skye perked up at the prospect of a trip out of the office. 'When are we going to Galloway?'

'That depends on your friend Fleming Carmichael. Probably within the next two or three weeks, but there's a lot to be done before then.'

Infinitely relieved that the worst of Lorimer's anger seemed to have dissipated into resignation, Skye spread her hands and beamed at him. 'Well? Where shall I start?'

Lorimer looked her over with a jaundiced eye. 'You can start by tidying yourself up. You look a complete mess.' He picked up his pen and reached for one of the files arranged in neat piles on his desk. 'I *had* planned to do some dictation, but it looks as if I'm going to have to write it all out by hand now. You can familiarise yourself with your office next door while I'm doing that, but make the most of it. After that, you're going to work!'

CHAPTER THREE

SKYE soon learnt that Lorimer Kingan was not a man of idle threats. She had never worked so hard in her life. Her previous employers had never expected very much of her, but Lorimer kept her busy all week, making her type and retype letters until they were perfect. Everything had to be immaculate, so that Skye, whose usual approach to work was slapdash in the extreme, found her desk piling high with plans to be photocopied and circulated, reports to be typed, letters to be filed and queries to be answered. It didn't take long to realise that if she didn't check absolutely everything it would just end up back on her desk with a sarcastic note scrawled across it and she would have to start all over again.

Nobody had ever made Skye work before, and by the end of every day she was so tired that she could hardly drag herself up the stairs to Vanessa's flat.

'You're just not used to doing a proper day's work,' said Vanessa unsympathetically. 'You'll get used to it.'

'That's what Lorimer said,' Skye grumbled that weekend. 'I thought at first that he was just trying to bully me into leaving of my own accord, but when I asked the others in the office they said he was like that all the time! They're all scared stiff of him. Can you believe it, Van? They never talk to each other! You walk into a room and there's dead silence. They've all got their heads down and they're *working*!'

Vanessa laughed at Skye's scandalised expression. 'People do, you know! How are they coping with you?

You must be a bit of a shock to the system there. You never *stop* talking.'

'I think they thought I was a bit mad at first, but they're all terribly nice once you get to know them. Of course, if Lorimer catches me chatting, he simply glowers! I told him he hadn't said anything about my taking a vow of silence, but he just looked down his nose at me in that infuriating way he has and told me I was there to work and not distract everyone else.' Skye scowled at the memory. 'You'd think I'd be allow five minutes off, wouldn't you? My fingers are worn to the bone retyping all those letters.'

'I thought you had a word processor?'

'I do, but I keep forgetting to save things so I have to type it all over again.' She sighed. 'I don't think I'm really cut out to be a secretary. I've already broken the photocopier and the coffee-machine and the phone's an absolute mystery to me. I cut one caller off five times when I was trying to put him through to Lorimer. In the end, I had to take the number and get Lorimer to call him back instead; he was furious.'

'I'm not surprised!'

'Well, I don't know why he can't have an ordinary phone like everyone else,' Skye complained. 'All those flashing lights just confuse me!'

Vanessa grinned at her friend. Skye was sprawled out in front of the electric fire, drinking gin and flicking idly through a glossy magazine. 'Do you still think Charles is worth it?'

Skye's fingers stilled and she stared unseeingly down at an advertisement for shoes so expensive she couldn't imagine how anyone could ever afford to buy them. 'Do you know,' she said slowly, 'I'd almost forgotten

Charles? Lorimer's kept me so busy I haven't had time to think about him.'

'You're obviously not that much in love with him, then.'

'Of course I am,' she protested mechanically, and then looked up at Vanessa with puzzled blue eyes. 'Aren't I?'

'If you ask me, you never have been,' said Vanessa firmly. 'I know he's good-looking, but you don't really know anything about him, do you? If he hadn't been so inaccessible, you'd never have given him another thought. As it was, he was a challenge, and, being you, you promptly decided you were madly in love with him, but really he's quite the wrong sort of man for you.'

'Oh, dear,' said Skye with a glum look. 'And I thought this was *it*. I must be terribly fickle. Do you think I'll ever fall in love properly, or will I end up a shrivelled old maid?'

'I don't think you need panic just yet,' said Vanessa drily, eyeing Skye's vivid face and slender loveliness. 'All you need is to find the *right* kind of man.'

'Yes, but where?'

'What about at work? This Lorimer Kingan sounds suitably masterful.'

Skye practically choked over her drink. 'Lorimer?' she spluttered.

'Why not?'

'Well, he's...he's...' Skye floundered, conscious of a strangely hollow feeling deep inside her. It was as if Vanessa's suggestion had opened a yawning black hole at her feet and she was afraid to look down in case she found what was waiting at the bottom of it.

'He's what?' said Vanessa, all innocence.

'He's insufferable! He's a bully. He's arrogant and grumpy and sarcastic and horrible. Honestly, Van, he treats me as if I were a five-year-old—and not a particularly bright one at that!'

Vanessa smiled smugly. 'He sounds perfect for you,' she said.

Fall in love with Lorimer! What a perfectly ridiculous idea! He was the last kind of man she was likely to fall for, Skye told herself huffily, but the more she tried to dismiss the idea, the more the memory of his mouth and his smile tugged at the edge of her mind with that queer stab of excitement. It left her feeling so cross and restless that Vanessa bullied her into a brisk walk up to the tip of Arthur's Seat on Sunday afternoon.

'What you need is a bit of exercise.'

Skye stood on the top of the crags and looked down at Edinburgh spread out below her. It was a chill, blowy day and the city had a grey, huddled look, as if crouching out of the cutting wind. Above it, the castle loomed gauntly out of its rock, impervious to the cold.

Turning up her collar against the wind, Skye shivered. She had been so convinced that Charles was all she wanted, but all it had taken was one light-hearted suggestion from Vanessa to turn all her ideas upside-down. There must be something wrong with her, she decided glumly. Vanessa was right. She was far too impetuous. No one else would have dreamt of chasing up to Edinburgh after a man she hardly knew, but she had gaily waved aside all objections. None of her friends liked Charles; that should have been a warning, but would she listen? No, she had just plunged into another fine mess, without thinking about anyone else who might be involved.

She had practically forced Lorimer into giving her the job, and all for what? Just so she could be near a man she now wasn't at all sure she really wanted. No wonder

Lorimer was so contemptuous of her! Skye sighed into the wind, remembering the exasperated expression he habitually wore whenever he looked at her. Perhaps she should just admit that she had been stupid and go back to London? Lorimer would probably be delighted.

Skye thought about leaving Edinburgh as they trudged down the hill and back across The Meadows, heads bent against the wind. She had been moaning about the job, but now that she thought about leaving it she found that she really quite liked being busy. Her previous bosses had all liked her, but thought her so hopeless that she had only ever been given mindless jobs to do before; Lorimer might not like her very much, but at least she hadn't had any time to be bored.

And she liked the other people at work: Sheila the receptionist, Murray the accountant, Lisa and Rab and Andrew in the marketing department ... it would be a shame to leave just as she was getting to know them all. Her mind flickered to Lorimer and then firmly away. She didn't want to think about how she would feel about not seeing him again.

Anxious to change the direction of her thoughts, Skye reminded herself of her father. As Fleming had predicted, he had been absolutely delighted to hear that she had found herself what he considered to a 'proper job' at long last. She suspected that he hadn't really believed her when she had vowed to stand on her own two feet, and it had been nice to show him that she had meant what she had said. Whatever happened, Charles had done her a favour in making her realise how spoilt she had always been. She had come to Edinburgh to change her life, and there was no reason why she shouldn't still do that. Deciding that she wasn't in love with Charles after all didn't mean that she had to disappoint her father and run home to carry on exactly as she had before. No, she owed her father more than that.

There was Vanessa to consider, too. If she left now, Vanessa would have to find someone else to share her flat, and Skye knew that she would miss her sturdy, practical friend. She would be reluctant to leave Edinburgh, too, she realised. In spite of the cold, the city had style. Much to her own surprise, Skye had found that she liked its dignified presence, the cobbled streets and the narrow closes and the smoky-grey light.

No, she wouldn't leave Edinburgh yet. She had been letting Vanessa's stupid suggestion get to her because she was tired, that was all. She should have just laughed it off, instead of letting herself imagine with quite such startling clarity just what it would be like to be in love with Lorimer, to be loved by him. She wished she wouldn't keep thinking about his mouth, about how it would feel against hers. How could she even consider the idea barely five minutes after being convinced that she was in love with Charles? Overwork, she told herself.

It would be stupid to make yet another impulsive decision. For once, Skye decided virtuously, she would think before she acted. She would see how she felt at the end of next week. Things might be different. She wouldn't let Lorimer work her so hard, and somehow she would arrange to meet Charles. Who knew? Face to face, all the old magic might come flooding back. It might have been silly to come here, but it would be even sillier to go without even giving Charles a chance.

'Stupid machine!' Skye kicked the photocopier in frustration. 'The engineer only came yesterday... you can't have broken already!' She jabbed at every button she could find, but the paper-jam symbol remained obstinately red. 'What's wrong with you?' she shouted, thumping the start button again. 'I've filled the paper tray, I've cleared the rollers, *now* what's the matter?'

The machine just sat there, dumb insolence written all over it, and Skye gave it another vindictive kick. 'There *is* no paper jam, you useless lump of metal! I've cleared it, so you can just *work*!'

'What on earth are you doing, Skye?' Lorimer's exasperated voice behind her made Skye swing round in confusion. He was standing in the doorway of her office, almost filling it with his massive frame, an expression of profound irritation on his face.

Skye's mouth dried at the sight of him. It had been the same all day yesterday, when she had been absurdly conscious of him. It was all Vanessa's fault, Skye thought crossly. If it hadn't been for that absurd suggestion, she would never have spent the whole of Monday noticing how broad his shoulders were, or how competent his hands. She wouldn't have noticed the pulse that beat in his throat or given a second thought to the way he rubbed his jaw when he was thinking. As it was, once she had started to notice, she couldn't stop noticing, and the odd sensation in the pit of her stomach whenever her eyes fell on his mouth left her feeling edgy and unusually irritable.

He had told her last night that he would be going straight to a meeting this morning, and she hadn't been expecting him in yet. Determined to show him that she could be efficient for once, she had planned to have all these reports beautifully copied and bound before he arrived, but the photocopier had refused to co-operate and now all she had done was manage to look foolish again.

She sighed. 'Your beastly photocopier is refusing to work.'

'It's a machine, Skye, not a monster,' said Lorimer testily. 'It's not *refusing*, it just hasn't been given the right instructions.'

'It's sulking,' Skye insisted, sulking, and aimed another kick at it.

'You're not going to get anywhere by kicking it or shouting at it,' Lorimer pointed out in a crisp voice. He dropped his briefcase on her desk and came over to push her firmly out of the way. 'This used to be a nice, quiet office before you came along. Now Princes Street seems like a haven of peace compared to having you around. Why do you have to make such a *fuss* about everything? You don't seem to be able to do anything quietly. You're either talking or laughing or ranting and raving at inanimate objects. I could hear you as soon as I came in the door!'

'You'd rant and rave if you had to deal with this machine,' said Skye bitterly. 'I don't know why people bother to have photocopiers. They're nothing but useless, expensive bits of machinery. They never work. They never do anything. They're not even pretty to look at! They just sit there wasting space, and as soon as you ask them to do a tiny bit of photocopying, which is what they're there for, they simply break down!'

'I'm surprised you don't identify with them,' said Lorimer with an ironic look. 'Expensive, useless, breaking down at the merest suggestion of work...it all sounds horribly familiar.' He glanced down at Skye's indignant face. 'You're much more decorative, I agree, but at least photocopiers aren't hopelessly distracting!'

'At least I work, which is more than you can say for this machine!' Skye said, bridling at the idea of being compared so unfavourably to a machine.

Lorimer gave a long-suffering sigh. 'What exactly is the problem?'

'I'm trying to collate these reports,' she said, pushing a few wayward curls away from her face. 'I was going to have them all ready for when you came back, and I was halfway through when the machine suddenly jammed. I cleared it all out, just like Sheila showed me, but now it won't start.'

'These machines are usually self-explanatory...' Lorimer frowned down at the panel of lights, while Skye peeked over his shoulder, longing to see him realise that he couldn't work it either. She watched as he read the instructions from start to finish and then pressed a button.

The machine promptly leapt into life.

'It did that deliberately!' Skye exploded. 'I've already tried that button!'

'It's all a matter of touch,' said Lorimer drily. 'It would be nice to think I could control *you* that easily.' Their heads were still bent together over the panel, and his eyes were very close. Skye looked into their dark blue depths and read exasperation and glimmering amusement and something else she couldn't identify, something that set her heart slamming painfully against her ribs. She was overwhelmingly conscious of the hard, unyielding strength of his body so near to hers, and her skin burned with a sudden urgent need to lean against him and feel his arms close about her.

Appalled at the way her thoughts were leading her, Skye stepped abruptly away from him. Lorimer straightened too, turning to look at her and then peer more closely as the jerk of her head set her earrings swinging wildly.

'What on earth have you got hanging from your ears?' he asked incredulously, reaching out to take one between his thumb and finger. '*Golf balls*?'

Skye was agonisingly aware of his fingers brushing her earlobe, of his warm hand near her throat. 'Do you like them?' she said huskily. Her pulse was drumming so loudly in her ears that she was hardly aware of what she was saying. It was if she could feel his glancing, impersonal touch with every fibre of her body. Even the pale blonde hair tangling softly over his fingers seemed to quiver with awareness.

'They certainly make a change from your usual menagerie,' Lorimer said. Skye loved eccentric jewellery and had an enormous collection of brightly painted wooden earrings which she wore with panache. 'So far we've had parrots, crocodiles, kangaroos and dolphins...I never know what's going to walk into the room every morning! What was it yesterday? Snakes?'

'Bananas,' Skye croaked, and to her enormous relief he let go of her earrings and stepped back. 'I saw these golf balls yesterday lunchtime,' she said, babbling with nerves. 'I couldn't resist them. I thought they'd be very appropriate for your PA.'

The look of amusement in Lorimer's eyes deepened. She had made an ineffectual attempt to keep the mop of pale gold curls away from her forehead with two plastic clips in the shape of a butterfly, and multi-coloured butterflies were appliquéd all over the huge peacock-blue sweatshirt she wore with bright green leggings. She looked vibrant and gaudy and utterly out of place.

'I can think of many words to describe your outfits, Skye,' he said, 'but "appropriate" is not one of them!'

'I suppose you'd like me in a sensible skirt, navy cardigan and pearl earrings?'

'It would be more restful than your usual wardrobe,' he agreed. 'It's like being in the same room as a firework that's about to go off.' Unexpectedly, he grinned. 'I keep waiting for the bang!'

Unprepared for the effect of his sudden smile, Skye's heart did a complete somersault and landed with a thump that took her breath away. It was the first time he had smiled properly at her; the brief glimpse of humour at that ill-fated interview was as nothing compared to the transformation now, as the stern mouth relaxed into a smile that showed strong white teeth and dissolved the severe angles of his face into warmth and humour and dazzling, dangerous charm.

'I—I'm afraid I haven't got any sensible clothes,' said Skye with a gasp, struggling to sound normal and terrified in case he would guess that a simple smile was enough to melt her bones and set every nerve in her body tingling.

'I didn't think you would have,' said Lorimer, still amused. 'Oh, well, I suppose we'll just have to get used to you the way you are.'

There was a pause, a sudden intensity in the air as, half reluctantly, Skye's eyes met his. They were so blue, so deep, a smile still lurking there. Could it be that Lorimer was beginning to accept her after all? The hope cheered her, and without thinking she smiled back at him, a warm, spontaneous smile that lit her whole face, but when she saw the expression that flared in Lorimer's eyes it faltered and faded. Had she been mistaken? She had been so glad at the idea that he might have begun to like her, but his expression was so strange now that she wasn't so sure.

Confused, she jerked her eyes away from his and cleared her throat. 'I'll—er—put these reports together, shall I?'

'Yes, I'd like them to go off today.' Lorimer moved away from the photocopier to let her lean down and collect the copies from the trays. When she straightened, clutching them to her chest, he was still watching her with that same odd expression in his eyes, but at her puzzled look he turned abruptly and went over to collect his briefcase from her desk.

As usual, it was covered in a litter of papers, files, dictionaries, manuals, maps and notebooks, interspersed with pens and emery boards, lipsticks and computer disks, bottles of Tippex and boxes of tissues and bars of chocolate. 'I don't know how you can work in this mess,' he said, surveying the clutter irritably. 'No wonder you keep losing things. And what are all these flowers doing here?' His gaze sharpened suddenly as he glanced at her. 'Are they from Charles Ferrars?'

'No.' Skye was amazed that the thought should even occur to him. 'I bought them.' She found that she was still breathlessly clutching the copies and relaxed her hold, relieved to be dealing with an astringent Lorimer again. He was so much more familiar like this, more familiar and much less disturbing than the warm, attractive man who had smiled at her so suddenly. In fact, he was so much like his usual self that she even began to wonder whether she had imagined the electric charge in the atmosphere as they stared at each other.

With an effort, Skye recovered her composure. 'Didn't you see the flowers on Sheila's desk? I bought some for Reception, some for in here and some for your office.' She threw open the door and showed him his desk, now resplendent with a huge vase full of Michaelmas daisies.

Lorimer looked at them and then at Skye as if she had gone mad. 'What for?' Yes, he was definitely back to normal.

'I thought it would make it all much cosier,' she explained. 'The office is so dull, I mean, it's all very tasteful,' she went on, glancing judiciously around the elegant, well-proportioned room, 'but it needs some warmth and colour, don't you think?'

Lorimer looked pointedly at the mass of flowers on her desk. 'A small vase of flowers is one thing, an entire herbaceous border is another. Was it necessary to get quite so many?'

'It seemed like a good idea at the time,' said Skye ingenuously. 'Besides, I got talking to the lady who runs the flower stall when I got off the bus this morning and I didn't feel I could walk off with one measly bunch of freesias. Her husband ran off years ago, and she's got five children to support, not to mention her old father who's got——'

'Spare me the details!' Lorimer held up a hand to interrupt her. 'I don't have your burning desire to discover the life history of every passing stranger. Just tell me whether you're planning to support this unfortunate woman every morning by buying out her entire stall.'

'Well, every other day is probably enough. Every morning seems a bit excessive.'

'I'm surprised that would stop you,' he said acidly. 'Excess seems to be your middle name. Am I expected to fund you in this charitable effort?'

'It wouldn't be that much,' she cajoled. 'And the office does look nicer, doesn't it?' Lorimer only grunted in reply. 'I asked Murray if I could claim it out of petty cash,' she perservered, 'and he said he was sure you wouldn't mind. He did say he'd have to check with you first, though,' she added quickly as Lorimer raised an eyebrow.

'I'm glad to hear it,' said Lorimer ironically, walking across to his desk and taking off his jacket before he sat down. 'You seem to have my accountant, as well as everybody else in this place, wrapped around your little finger. Sheila's just been telling me that you're organising some kind of staff outing this evening.'

'We're just going out for a pizza. I thought it would be nice to get to know everyone socially.' Skye hesitated in the doorway, watching him roll up his shirt-sleeves as he looked down at the collection of messages she had left on his desk. 'Do you want to come?'

Lorimer looked up at that, dark brows raised. 'Me?'

'Well, you are a member of staff,' she pointed out.

His eyes rested thoughtfully on her for a moment, and then he returned his attention to the messages. 'Thank you, but no, thank you. I already have plans for this evening.'

'Oh.' Skye felt a little foolish. Of course he would have his own plans. He would have much better things to do than go for a pizza. She wondered what he would be doing, whom he would be with. 'Er, would you like a cup of coffee?'

'Thank you,' said Lorimer absently without looking up from the messages.

Skye went downstairs to the little kitchen in the basement where she found Sheila refilling the percolator. 'I'm really looking forward to this evening,' she receptionist said eagerly. 'We never thought about going out before you came, Skye. Everyone just used to go home after work, and we hardly talked to each other even when we were here. I don't know why, but everything's been more fun since you came.'

Wandering over to the window, Skye peered up through railings at the street and the headless legs walking past. It was a damp grey day and the lights had been on in all the offices since early that morning. 'I asked Lorimer if he wanted to come along this evening,' she said casually and Sheila nearly dropped the tin of coffee.

'You didn't!'

'Why not?'

'I wouldn't have dared,' whispered Sheila, impressed. 'You are brave, Skye! I'd be terrified of him if he shouted at me the way he shouts at you.'

'I usually deserve it,' said Skye with a frank grin. 'Anyway he's not coming, so you can relax. He said he was busy.'

'Probably,' Sheila agreed in relief. She began spooning the coffee into the filter. 'I think he goes out quite a lot.'

Skye fiddled with the mugs. 'Who with? Has he got a girlfriend?'

'I don't know. He's rather private, isn't he? I've seen him leaving with Moira Lindsay a couple of times. She's lovely, and they say she plays golf beautifully.'

'Moira Lindsay?' The name rang a bell in Skye's mind. 'Isn't she the girl who's going to take over as Lorimer's secretary after Christmas?'

Sheila nodded. 'That's right. Apparently she's very good. It'll be funny without you, though, Skye. You've only been here a week and already it's hard to remember what it was like before you came.'

Skye hardly heard her. She found that she was gripping Lorimer's mug so tightly that her knuckles were white, and she put it back on the bench with a sharp click. No wonder Lorimer couldn't wait for these three months to be over so that Moira could come and work for him! How cosy to have his girlfriend and his secretary all rolled into one! He had told her that Moira was exceptionally well-qualified, but she hadn't appreciated then just how qualified he meant, she thought bitterly.

She was rather quiet as she walked back up the stairs with Sheila, taking the two mugs from the tray as they reached the top. It was just as well she had found out about Moira before she had a chance to do anything silly like falling for Lorimer after all.

Setting her own mug down amid the clutter on her desk, she carried the other carefully into Lorimer's office. It was very full and her tongue stuck out in concentration as she tried not to slop any of the hot liquid over her hand.

She was halfway across the room when she glanced up to find Lorimer watching her with the same peculiar expression in his eyes that she had seen there before. She stopped, puzzled, and he looked hastily away to pick up his pen.

'If you didn't fill the mug up to the brim, you might find it easier to carry,' he said, but Skye had the feeling that he was almost forcing himself to sound irritated. She leant over the plans spread over his desk to hand him the mug.

'Careful, it's hot,' she warned as he made to take it from her, and he moved his hand round over hers to take the handle. The feel of his skin against hers sent such an unexpected jolt of response through her that she flinched as if she had been stung, and the hot coffee came surging over the rim of the mug on to her fingers.

'Aagh!' Instinctively, she whipped her hand away before Lorimer had proper hold of the mug, and it fell with a crack on to the pristine plans, sloshing coffee everywhere.

'You stupid woman!' Lorimer thrust back his chair and leapt to his feet before the coffee had a chance to stream into his lap. There was nothing forced about his irritation now! 'What did you let go for?'

Skye sucked at her scalded fingers. 'I thought my hand was more important than your plan!'

'That's a matter of judgement!' he said furiously. 'Look at the mess you've made! All these plans will have to be copied again.' He scrumpled them up together with the coffee and deposited them in the bin while Skye mopped ineffectually at the remaining puddles with some tissues. 'Here, give me those,' he said, snatching them out of her hand. 'You're just making things worse as usual!'

'I don't know why you're so cross with me,' said Skye. 'It was an accident.'

'There are too many "accidents" when you're around,' he snapped. 'Everything you do ends up a shambles. You've only got to look at something for it to break down. The office has been totally chaotic since you arrived, I've got work piling up because you're so slow, you spend your time distracting my staff so nobody's getting any work done and you're so inefficient, you can't even take a message properly!'

'What do you mean?'

'Look at these!' He picked up the sheaf of messages she had left him earlier, now rather damp and coffee-stained, and shook them at her. 'Half of them are illegible, the other half are so vague as to be unintelligible. You haven't put a date or a time on any of them, you haven't taken any numbers so that I can call these people back and you do *not* spell Kirkcudbright K-E-R-K-double O-B-R-Y!'

'I only spelt it how it sounds,' Skye objected.

'You ought to be able to spell it properly!'

'It's not my fault if half the towns in Scotland choose to have stupid spellings,' she muttered. 'You'd need to be telepathic to know how to spell all of them.'

'All you'd need is a reference book,' said Lorimer icily. 'And a modicum of intelligence, of course—obviously the biggest problem where you are concerned.' He threw the sodden tissues in the bin. 'And you have the nerve to complain about photocopiers being a waste of space! At least they don't throw coffee all over you!'

'Why don't you employ a robot, then?' snapped Skye, losing her temper. 'You'd like that, wouldn't you? A soulless machine you could shout at to your heart's content and it would never answer back!'

'I wouldn't need to shout at a secretary who had the smallest claim to competence!'

'Well, you can save your lungs in future,' said Skye angrily. 'You don't need to shout at me any more. I'm leaving!' Whirling round, she stalked to the door. 'You can type your own letters till your precious Moira gets here!' she told him, and went out, slamming the door behind her.

CHAPTER FOUR

PERILOUSLY close to tears, Skye began scrabbling around on her desk and throwing her possessions into her bag. He was a pig! An arrogant, obnoxious pig! She hated him! How could she have come so dangerously near to liking him just because he smiled at her? She must have been mad.

The memory of Lorimer's smile was so strong that Skye froze in the act of reaching out for her lipstick. Slowly, she sank back into her chair and stared at the flowers she had bought that morning with a perplexed expression. It wasn't like her to get so upset. She had a naturally sunny nature and criticism usually rolled over her unnoticed, but somehow it had been different today. Lorimer's comments had caught her on the raw. *Was* she really that hopeless? Was that why she suddenly cared? Or was it just disappointment at realising that she had been fooling herself when she thought that Lorimer might like her in spite of everything?

Would she have been quite so upset if she hadn't just learnt about his relationship with Moira Lindsay?

Skye fumbled for a tissue and blew her nose. Why should she care? It was no business of hers what Lorimer did in his spare time, after all. She had made enough of a fool of herself falling in love with one unsuitable, inaccessible man without doing the same thing all over again. No, that was the last thing she needed. What she needed was not to be in love with anyone for a while. Instead, she wanted to try and do a proper job for a change... and she wasn't going about it the right way, she realised honestly. Shouting at her boss and over-reacting to criticism that was all too justified was hardly the behaviour of a dedicated PA.

Looking around her office, Skye accepted that she didn't want to leave, no matter what she had said to Lorimer. For once in her life, she had found a job that she enjoyed. It would be stupid to storm out because of a few angry words. Charles was irrelevant now; what mattered was her father. Only last night she had spoken to him on the phone, and assured him that he didn't need to worry about her any longer, that she was still determined to make a success of the job. She *couldn't* disappoint him now, especially not when her elder brother had rung her later to confide that their father was having business problems. Skye felt vaguely guilty when she realised that it was the first time any of her brothers had thought to tell her anything like that. In the past they must have assumed that she was too frivol-ous to understand or care. Her brother's news had strengthened her determination not to add to her father's worries. She had been a bad enough daughter as it was. Skye sniffed and blew her nose again.

She looked at the door to Lorimer's office. He was probably in there rubbing his hands at the thought of getting rid of her. She wouldn't blame him if he refused to have any more to do with her, but she could only ask him for another chance. The worst he could do was say no.

Squaring her shoulders, Skye gave her nose a final blow, pushed back her chair and got to her feet. She hesitated by the door, and then knocked.

It was opened so suddenly that Lorimer could only have been standing right behind it. For a moment, they stared at each other in silence, her hand still raised from the knock. Sky's nose was rather pink. Her mouth was still tremulous and her eyes had the shimmering look of unshed tears, but her chin was tilted at a proud angle. She wondered what he had been doing behind the door.

'Well?' he said at last.

'I wanted to apologise,' said Skye a little uncertainly. Her hand dropped to her side. Everything always seemed easy until Lorimer's unsettling eyes were on her. 'You were right, I'm a hopeless secretary but I really will try harder if you'll give me another chance.'

'You want to stay?'

'Yes.'

There was a tiny pause. Lorimer's eyes held an odd, unreadable expression. 'If you must know,' he admitted at last, 'I was on my out to apologise to you.'

'You were?' Skye looked at him in surprise.

'I shouldn't have spoken to you like that. I was thinking about...' he hesitated '...something else, and wasn't expecting to have hot coffee poured all over me. I'm afraid I took my bad temper out on you. You were right, it was an accident.' Suddenly, he reached out and took her hand, turning it up so that he could inspect her fingers. 'Were you badly burnt?'

'N-no.' Skye found herself stammering, so conscious was she of the touch of his hand. 'Not really.'

He was looking down at her hand, his thumb rubbing almost absently over her palm. 'Sure?'

'Y-yes.' She took a deep breath, hardly knowing whether to be relieved or disappointed when he dropped her hand. 'I'm sorry about your plans.'

'They can be copied again. Perhaps you could do them this afternoon?'

'You mean I can stay?'

Lorimer tried to look stern. 'Well, it would save me finding another secretary,' he said. 'It would take me at least another two weeks before I could find anyone to replace you, and even at your speed of typing you could get quite a lot done in that time.'

Skye told herself that she ought to be grateful, but Lorimer wasn't deceived by her determinedly humble expression, and a reluctant half-smile bracketed his mouth. 'Oh, all right,' he said, shoving his hands in his trouser pockets. 'I'll admit it. You may be absolutely infuriating, but you do get the job done eventually in your own funny way, and I suppose that in spite of it all I'm getting used to you.'

He was getting used to her! It might not be the most effusive compliment in the world, but it was a start. Skye felt suddenly ridiculously happy.

'I really *will* try and be more efficient,' she assured him, and this time he smiled properly, shaking his head in mock-exasperation.

'Quite frankly, Skye, you're trying enough already!' He turned back to his desk, once more his astringent self. 'Now that we've sorted that out, can we get on with some work?'

'Of course.' Skye beamed at him, feeling as if she'd had a last-minute reprieve from some terrible fate. 'Shall I get you some more coffee?'

'Thank you,' he said drily, settling himself behind his desk. 'Perhaps a tray would be a good idea this time?'

Skye closed the door on him, still smiling idiotically, just as the phone began to ring. She stood with her hand on the receiver for a moment, reluctant to pick it up, wanting to remember instead the way he had smiled, the touch of his hand...

The telephone shrilled insistently beneath her hand and she picked it up with a sigh, unable to ignore it any longer. 'Hello?'

'Skye?'

'Yes?' she said blankly.

'It's Charles . . . Charles Ferrars.'

'Oh . . . Charles . . . hello.' A week ago she would have been breathless with excitement at the very sound of his voice; now she didn't even recognise it. There was definitely something wrong with her.

'You sound a bit vague, Skye.' Was it her imagination, or was there a peevish note in his voice at her lack of enthusiasm? 'Are you all right?'

'I'm fine.' Skye made an effort to sound bright. 'Did you want to talk to Lorimer?'

'Eventually, yes, but I thought it would be nice to have a little chat with you first. I've been talking to Fleming about you...I didn't realise you knew him quite so well.'

Was that why he was suddenly being so friendly? Skye hated herself for being so cynical. 'I thought you knew,' she said. 'We met at one of his parties, after all.'

'Yes, but there were so many people there. I thought you were just an acquaintance.'

'No, Fleming and Marjorie are practically family. Marjorie's my godmother.'

'So Fleming was telling me.' Charles's voice was smooth and assured. 'We didn't have much of a chance to talk the other day. What about lunch tomorrow?'

It was the invitation she had longed for. 'I can't tomorrow, I'm afraid,' said Skye. 'I've already arranged to meet Vanessa for lunch.'

There was a tiny pause, as if Charles was waiting for her to say that she would cancel her date with Vanessa so that she could see him instead. 'What about tomorrow evening, then?' he suggested at last. 'I'm hoping to come in and see Lorimer anyway, so we could go on after you finish work.'

'All right.' Skye wished she felt more enthusiastic about the idea. She would rather have met Charles away from the office—away from Lorimer's penetrating blue eyes—but she couldn't think of a good reason to refuse. Besides, she *had* decided to give her original plan a chance. Perhaps when she saw Charles again all the old attraction would come flooding back? 'I'll see you tomorrow, then. Now, shall I put you through to Lorimer?'

Lorimer, when told who wanted to speak to him, sounded suddenly hard. 'Ferrars? Oh, yes, I'd forgotten just why you're so keen to stay here. For a moment there, I really thought you wanted the job.' He gave a short, bitter laugh. 'Stupid of me.'

Skye bit her lip. She would have liked to tell Lorimer that she hadn't given Charles a thought when she asked him to let her stay, but he was hardly likely to believe her, not after the way she had prattled on about following Charles to Edinburgh. What an idiot he must have thought her! What an idiot she had *been*. She should never have told Lorimer the whole story. Now he would never believe the real reason she had wanted to stay. Skye wasn't at all sure she knew what it was anyway.

'I'd better speak to him, I suppose,' Lorimer went on impatiently when she said nothing. 'Put him through.'

She put the phone down, feeling strangely flat, and went slowly down to the kitchen to get him some more coffee. When she came back, Lorimer was scowling ferociously down at a letter and making savage notes in the margin. This time, she didn't risk handing him the mug, but set it carefully down on the desk.

'I gather he's taking you out tomorrow,' said Lorimer snappishly, without looking up from the letter.

'We're just going out for a drink,' she said, and then wondered why she sounded as if she was apologising. It wasn't any of Lorimer's business what she did after work.

'Well, don't forget what I told you about confidentiality,' he said nastily. 'I don't want Charles Ferrars knowing everything that goes on here.'

Skye looked down at his dark head, puzzled. 'Why should he be interested?'

'Why else would he be taking you out?' Lorimer retorted, lifting his head to watch her almost accusingly.

'Is it beyond the bounds of possibility that he might actually want to see *me*?' Skye's voice was sugar-sweet but there was a spark of anger in her eyes. They'd had one argument today already and she'd thought they'd made their peace. Now Lorimer seemed determined to pick another one.

'I know Ferrars' type. They always have an ulterior motive. He might be interested in Kingan Associates, or he might be interested in currying favour with Fleming Carmichael, but he's not interested in you or your beautiful blue eyes.'

Skye felt like picking up his mug and pouring coffee all over him all over again. Her chin tilted defiantly. 'Well, we'll see, won't we?'

Blue eyes met blue in unspoken challenge, and then Lorimer turned back to his letter with a grim smile. 'Yes, we'll see.'

*   *   *

'You didn't tell me how gorgeous he was!' Vanessa sent Skye an accusing look as they walked down the steps from the office the next day.

'Who?' said Skye unconvincingly.

'Your boss, of course!' Lorimer had been in the hall talking to Murray as Vanessa and Skye left the office for lunch. He had broken off his conversation with the accountant to remind Skye that she only had an hour off.

'I know you have an extremely flexible approach to time-keeping,' he had said without bothering to disguise his sarcasm, 'but perhaps you could make an effort to be back on time today? I've got a lot to get done this afternoon and you're not swanning off with Charles Ferrars until it's finished.'

He had been in a nit-picking mood all morning and Skye had been unable to do anything right. She had gritted her teeth and reminded herself of her father, but if it hadn't been for him she would have been sorely tempted to tell Lorimer Kingan what he could do with his rotten job. She had begun to think that she had imagined that brief moment of warmth and understanding that had flared between them yesterday before Charles had telephoned.

Not that it could have been that that had put Lorimer in such a bad mood, Skye reasoned. Moira Lindsay had rung only that morning, and Skye's heart had sunk unaccountably at the sound of the other girl's low, musical voice and pleasant manner. Lorimer hadn't taken out his bad temper on *her*. Instead he had sounded delighted to hear from her, and as soon as he had put the phone down he'd been on to Skye, telling her to book a table for two at one of Edinburgh's most exclusive restaurants.

Skye sighed as she and Vanessa crossed Charlotte Square. So what if he wanted to take Moira out? She had already decided she was going to concentrate on making a success of her job and on not being involved with anyone for a while, and very happy she was too.

'I'm not surprised you lost interest in Charles once you met Lorimer,' Vanessa was saying, buttoning up her coat against the wind.

'I haven't lost interest in Charles,' Skye said, only too aware of the half-hearted note in her voice. 'Not exactly. I'm just... playing it cool. You were the one who suggested I should do that, after all.'

'Oh, come on, Skye. I've only had a glimpse of Lorimer, but that was enough to tell that he's twice the man Charles is. I'm not surprised you keep getting things wrong. If my boss looked like that, I wouldn't be able to concentrate on my work either. That rugged look is terribly attractive, isn't it? Much more so than Charles's smooth good looks. His charm's all on the surface with nothing underneath.'

'At least he's got charm, which is more than I can say for Lorimer,' snapped Skye, conveniently forgetting how devastating his smile had been and concentrating instead on how grumpy and disagreeable he had been that morning.

'You're not your usual sunny self, Skye,' Vanessa commented with a searching look. 'Is there something you're not telling me?'

'Of course not.' Skye kicked through a pile of fallen leaves and avoided her friend's eye. She did feel oddly edgy and unsettled but it had nothing to do with Lorimer taking Moira out tonight, absolutely nothing. The trouble was, she didn't know *how* she felt any more. She had never reacted to anyone quite the way she had to

Lorimer. There was something about him that threw her off balance. Whenever she had met an attractive man before, she and her friends had enjoyed discussing every nuance of the relationship in exhaustive detail. It had all been part of the fun, so much so that sometimes the man in question was less entertaining than talking about him. Lorimer was different. For a start, they didn't *have* a relationship to discuss, and even if they had Skye knew instinctively that she wouldn't want to giggle about it over a bottle of wine.

No, she couldn't tell Vanessa how she felt about Lorimer. There was nothing *to* tell.

'Of course not,' she said again more firmly, and spent the rest of the lunch-hour being determinedly cheerful at the prospect of seeing Charles again.

Lorimer was, if anything, even more bad-tempered that afternoon, and, in spite of Skye's arriving back from lunch five minutes early, was so scathing about a report she had spent hours typing that she could cheerfully have hit him. Moira was welcome to him, she decided furiously, stomping out of his office and shutting the door behind her with unnecessary force.

Turning from the door, she found herself suddenly face to face with Charles, who rose from a chair near her desk.

'I'm a little early for my appointment, I know,' he said smoothly. 'I asked your receptionist if I could wait in here for you. I hope you don't mind?' He smiled at her in a way that had once had her weak at knees, but which now left her feeling nothing other than surprised that he had arrived so early. The Charleses of this world usually liked to give the impression they were rushing from one important meeting to another.

'Of course I don't mind,' she said. Her mind was still half on Lorimer's unreasonableness, her face vivid with suppressed anger, but she gave Charles a brilliant smile, largely because she knew Lorimer wouldn't like it. 'I'm sorry you've had to wait here alone. I didn't realise you were here.'

She had forgotten how handsome Charles was. His fair hair was beautifully cut and he was dressed as usual with impeccable taste in an elegant grey suit and discreet tie. He might have been a model, standing there with his perfect features and his perfect teeth and his perfect tan. Only the peculiarly cold eyes gave him an individual look. Skye gazed at him, hoping against hope that she would fall in love with him all over again, but her heart continued to beat steadily, undisturbed.

Realising that she was behaving in a very distracted manner, Skye walked across and kissed him on the cheek. 'It's lovely to see you again, Charles,' she said, much more warmly than she would have done if Lorimer hadn't been so thoroughly unpleasant.

'It's good to see you too, Skye.' Charles held on to her a little longer than necessary. 'I hadn't realised quite how good it would be.'

'I hate to break up this touching reunion,' said Lorimer acidly behind them, 'but you've still got work to do, Skye. You don't finish work until five-thirty.'

Skye was furious with herself for the guilty way she jumped away from Charles at the sound of his voice. Lorimer moved forward to greet the other man with ill-concealed hostility, and Skye couldn't help remembering how Vanessa had compared the two of them. Charles was cool and smooth, sophisticated and assured in his tailored suit, while Lorimer, in a tweed jacket that only seemed to emphasise his rugged quality, was massive and granite-hard and gave off an unmistakable aura of suppressed fury. When the two men shook hands, they reminded Skye of two dogs, circling aggressively, their hackles rising in instinctive distrust.

They disappeared into Lorimer's office and Skye, still smarting from Lorimer's comments, set about correcting the report, thumping the keyboard resentfully with angry fingers that only created more mistakes. By the time they emerged, she was in just as bad a mood as Lorimer and had somehow resolved not to give Lorimer another thought at the same time as showing him just what he was missing that evening.

Lorimer opened the door just in time to see her touching up her lipstick and his expression hardened. Skye quickly snapped her mirror closed and dropped the lipstick into her bag, directing a dazzling smile over Lorimer's shoulder at Charles.

'Finished?'

'Obviously,' Lorimer answered for him sourly. 'More to the point, have *you* finished?'

'Of course.' Skye was the picture of virtue. She glanced at her watch. 'Oh, dear, it's only twenty seven minutes past five. Charles, would you mind terribly waiting three minutes? I don't want Lorimer to think I'm deserting my post.'

'You'd better go if you're so anxious to leave,' Lorimer snapped, goaded.

He stood looking thunderous as Skye graciously allowed Charles to help her into her coat. 'I can't tell you how much I've been looking forward to this,' she said, smiling sweetly up at him and delighted to see, when she risked a glance at Lorimer, that his black look had deepened. Evidently unable to bear the sight of her simpering up at Charles any longer, he gave a contemptuous snort and slammed back into his office without a word of farewell.

Satisfied, Skye lifted her eyebrows in mock surprise and turned a bright smile on Charles. 'Shall we go?'

He took her to a wine bar behind Hanover Street. 'I'm sorry I haven't been in touch with you sooner, Skye,' he said, pouring her a glass of wine. 'But it's been frantically busy... you know how it is.'

Two weeks ago she hadn't known what busy was, Skye reflected, but she smiled and took the glass. 'I know what you mean. We're busy too.'

'Not too busy, I hope,' said Charles, edging closer. 'It would be nice to see more of you since we're both exiles up here. It's quite a coincidence you being here at the same time, isn't it?'

'Yes, isn't it?' said Skye with a weak smile, wondering if there was any way he could have guessed that she had simply followed him. Now she couldn't imagine what had possessed her. What had she seen in him? He was very good-looking, of course, and she could see several women in the wine bar casting her envious looks, but somehow he had seemed so much more attractive when he didn't want anything to do with her. Vanessa was right. All Charles had been was a challenge, and now that he was sitting beside her, toasting her with his glass and saying that he wanted to see more of her, all she could feel was ashamed that she could have made so much fuss about a man who couldn't make her pulse beat anything more than sluggishly. She couldn't help comparing him to Lorimer, who only had to look at her to send her pulse into orbit and set her heart lurching out of control.

'So how are you enjoying working for Lorimer Kingan?' Charles asked. Even the sound of Lorimer's name was enough to make her heart jump. 'Tough character, isn't he? Pity he's such a rabid Scot.'

'He was badly let down by an English firm recently,' said Skye before she could stop herself. Heavens, who was she to leap to Lorimer's defence?

Charles shrugged. 'Development's a tough business. If you ask me, the Scots are too damned sentimental to make good businessmen.'

'I wouldn't call Lorimer sentimental!' Skye stared at him in astonishment.

'Oh, he looks formidable enough, I know, but I can't help feeling that he *cares* a bit too much about what he's doing.' Charles made caring sound like some form of aberration. 'He won't accept that the bottom line is money.'

Skye took a defiant gulp of her wine. 'And it is for you?'

'I'm honest about it,' said Charles carelessly. 'Fleming's brought me up here to try and drag the Edinburgh office into the twentieth century. All I need to do is show them how to pull off a really profitable deal, and I can hotfoot it back to London. The sooner the better as far as I'm concerned.'

'Don't you like it up here?' Skye looked at him curiously, and he gave an exaggerated shudder.

'It's a barbaric country! And Edinburgh's so cold and *dull*! I'd have thought you of all people would understand, Skye. You've always struck me as a real London girl.'

'I used to think I was,' she said slowly. 'But I'm not so sure now. I like Edinburgh. I think it's a wonderful city.'

Charles's expression was half patronising, half pitying. 'You've changed.'

'Yes,' said Skye. 'I think I have.'

The evening seemed to drag. Skye, who would normally have been in her element sitting thigh to thigh with a handsome man in a cosy wine bar, kept glancing surreptitiously at her watch and wondering what Lorimer and Moira were doing. Were they toying with their food, smiling at each other over the candlelight, planning how wonderful life would be once Moira had replaced Skye and they could spend all day together?

Skye drank her wine desperately and told herself for the umpteenth time that she didn't care. She tried to concentrate on Charles, but found herself increasingly surprised that she had ever found anything to like about him at all. Why on earth had she gone to so much trouble for him? She thought of the dinner parties she had arranged, the invitations she had wangled, the elaborate charades she had got herself involved just so that she would see him. Now she could only wonder at herself.

She was also beginning to have a nasty suspicion that Lorimer had been right when he had claimed that Charles was more interested in Kingan Associates and her closeness to the Carmichaels than in her. He asked an awful lot of questions about Lorimer's business which Skye parried by pretending to be more interested in him. As this meant listening to a diatribe about the parochial attitudes in Fleming's Edinburgh office, the climate, the lack of social life and, obviously more important as far as Charles was concerned, the lack of opportunities to make big money, she was soon bored and increasingly aware of how his cut-crystal tones carried through the chatter of the wine bar.

Skye's smile grew rigid, but fortunately her sense of humour came to her rescue before she did anything she might regret. This dreadful evening served her right!

Edging as far away from Charles as she could, Skye reminded herself again of evenings spent hanging around in his favourite wine bar, hoping that he would appear. If she could have imagined her present lack of enthusiasm then, she could have saved herself an awful lot of trouble! She could have stayed in London... Skye contemplated her wine and thought about how different her life would have been. She would never have come to Edinburgh. She would never have learnt what it was to work hard. She would never have met Lorimer.

Perhaps things hadn't turned out so badly after all.

She left as soon as she could. By the time she had given Vanessa a blow-by-blow account of her ghastly evening and both girls had enjoyed a good giggle, Skye had accepted that she had made a complete and utter fool of herself over Charles and felt immeasurably better. From now on, she told Vanessa, she was going to dedicate herself to work.

Ignoring Vanessa's hoots of incredulous laughter, Skye mapped out an optimistic future. She would concentrate on her job so that when Lorimer's precious Moira was free, she would have some decent experience to find a proper job somewhere else. She would make her father proud of her after all. What she *wouldn't* do was waste any more time thinking about men. She had learnt her lesson with Charles. There was no point in falling for men who patently weren't interested in her—and that included Lorimer Kingan! No, from now on, work would be her watchword.

CHAPTER FIVE

'YOU don't mind socialising with your boss, do you dear?'

'Of course not,' said Skye automatically. She fiddled with her telephone cord and wondered what it would be like to see Lorimer outside the office. 'I'd have thought it would be more a case of whether *he* minded or not.'

'Nonsense,' said Marjorie Carmichael robustly. 'A pretty girl like you? Of course he won't mind. The thing is,' she went on confidentially, 'Fleming feels that Lorimer and Charles aren't getting on very well together, and he thought it might help for them to meet on a social basis for a change. I'm afraid it's mixing business with pleasure for you, dear, but we did so want to see you, and you're always such good company at a dinner party.'

Skye laughed. 'I'll try my best.'

'I knew I could rely on you, dear. Till next Saturday, then? Is half-past seven all right?'

'That'll be fine. See you then.' Skye put the phone down thoughtfully. She had seen little of Lorimer over the last few days. He had been in and out to meetings, and yesterday he had spent the whole day in Perth discussing a possible new site. He hadn't suggested that she go with him. The atmosphere between them had been strained ever since Charles had taken her out for that drink and Skye was glad she had decided to devote herself to her work instead of any foolish daydreams about Lorimer coming to like her in time. It was perfectly obvious that he found her as exasperating as ever, although she really *had* been trying to be more efficient.

Now she couldn't help wondering if he might change his mind if he saw her away from the office. This might be her opportunity to show him that she wasn't just a muddle-headed secretary. She would be glamorous, sophisticated, a woman of the world. The prospect sent a thrill of anticipation prickling down her spine. Skye sternly repressed the feeling, reminding herself of her decision not to get involved with any more inaccessible men, but still, it *would* be nice to show him that she wasn't quite as stupid as he thought.

One lunch-hour, she sneaked out and, feeling rather guilty at spending so much money on a simple desire to impress someone she had already decided she wasn't going to bother trying to impress, she spent almost all her monthly salary on a classic little black dress. Skye had never owned anything so plain, so simple or so stunning before. The dress was unrelieved black, relying on its cut and its fabric to make its effect. It had short sleeves and an off-the-shoulder V-neck that threw her fine skin into relief and emphasised the pure line of her clavicle.

Skye even impressed herself when she looked into the mirror on Saturday evening. There was no doubt about it, she did look different.

'I thought you'd given up on Charles?' Vanessa eyed Skye suspiciously as she peacocked in front of the long mirror in the hall.

'I have.'

'Then why are going to so much effort for tonight?'

Skye made a great show of adjusting the black dress over her shoulders and kept her eyes firmly fixed on the mirror. Why *was* she going to so much effort? 'I just thought it would make a change,' she said, airily enough, and changed the subject quickly. 'Can you lend me some earrings, Van? I think the parrots would spoil the effect.'

Eventually they decided on a pair of huge, heavy gold knots that caught the light and looked suitably dramatic with her shining hair piled on top of her head. A few wayward curls kept escaping down her neck, but Vanessa said firmly that it didn't matter. 'It makes you look softer—less drop-dead sophisticated.'

'Do I really look sophisticated?' Skye regarded her reflection in delight.

'I never thought I'd say it, but yes, you do.' Vanessa studied her friend as if she'd never seen her before. 'You've always been much too pretty for your own good, but I've never known you look beautiful before. Are you sure you're not still trying to impress Charles?'

'Absolutely sure.' Skye wasn't quite ready to admit, even to herself, that it was Lorimer she was trying to impress but as she smoothed down her dress nervously on Fleming's doorstep she couldn't help wondering if he would think she was beautiful too. She tried to compose her face into a glamorous, world-weary expression to go with the dress, but it was hard trying to look mysterious when you were being greeted by people who had known you since you were in nappies.

Fleming swept her into a hug that left her pink and laughing, and by the time Marjorie had emerged to give her an affectionate kiss there was little left of her decorous image. 'My goodness, you do look pretty,' said Marjorie, ushering Skye into the sitting-room. 'Now, come in and meet...'

Skye hardly heard what she said. She had stopped dead on the threshold as she found herself staring across the room at Lorimer. He was standing by the fireplace, holding a glass of whisky in one hand, and as Skye came in he looked up. She had been expecting to see him, of course, but she was unprepared for how much the severity of the dinner-jacket and tie suited him without detracting in the slightest from the aura of toughness that was so much part of him. He looked solid and decisive and devastatingly attractive, and Skye felt the breath leak out of her.

Across the room, her eyes met his, and for a moment as they looked at each other it was as if he had been caught off guard and his expression flared with something that looked almost like shock, and something else too, something deeper and far more disturbing. His eyes shuttered almost immediately, but it left Skye feeling jarred and oddly shaken.

'You remember Charles, of course.' Marjorie was at her elbow and Skye pulled herself together with an effort. Charles was looking handsome but somehow diminished standing next to Lorimer and Skye, aware of Lorimer's eyes on her, greeted him warmly with a kiss on both cheeks. Over his shoulder, she could see Lorimer's expression tighten.

'No need to introduce you to Lorimer, I know,' Marjorie chattered on, 'but you won't know Moira... Moira Lindsay.'

For the first time, Skye registered the presence of a girl standing beside Lorimer. She had a coolly serene presence that didn't make her immediately noticeable, but when she looked closer Skye saw that she had fresh clear skin and beautiful red hair, and her heart sank. Moira had the sort of radiance and composure that came from truly healthy living. Sky thought guiltily of the self-indulgent evenings she spent with Vanessa, drinking gin and eating chocolate and crisps and ice-cream. Why couldn't she be the sort of girl that would far rather spend her weekends running around some sports field than lying in front of the television?

Skye wasn't surprised that Lorimer was so enthusiastic about Moira. She was obviously intelligent, attractive, fit and, worst of all, she was *nice*. Fully prepared to dislike her on sight, Skye found that she simply couldn't. Moira was friendly without being in the least bit patronising.

'I'm delighted to meet you at last,' she said to Skye. 'I've heard a lot about you.'

'Oh, dear,' said Skye and glanced involuntarily at Lorimer who was watching her sardonically.

Moira laughed. 'Don't worry, if you've got any dreadful secrets, Lorimer isn't telling. He certainly didn't tell me how glamorous you were!'

Skye warmed to her even more, but before she could reply Lorimer interposed, 'She doesn't usually look like this. There's nothing glamorous about the parrots and bananas she's usually decked out in. I hardly recognised when you walked in looking so plain, but as soon as I saw those over-the-top earrings I realised it was you after all.'

'They're not over the top!' said Skye, offended. So much for impressing Lorimer with her new-found sophistication! His acid comments made her feel awkward and silly, like a little girl dressed up in her mother's clothes. Her blue eyes were hostile as she touched the earrings defensively.

'They're enormous,' he contradicted her. 'They must be agony.'

'Rubbish,' lied Skye. The clips were pinching and dragging on her lobes with the weight of the knots, but she wasn't going to admit that to Lorimer.

He was patently unconvinced by her denial anyway. He glanced meaningfully at Charles. 'The lengths some girls will go to get their man,' he said so that only Skye could hear.

Skye's chin came up. If Lorimer wanted to think she was still interested in Charles, so much the better. Anything was better than him even suspecting that the effort had been not for Charles's benefit but for his. She turned deliberately away and began flirting very obviously with Charles.

She felt miserable and confused. Bitterly, she realised how badly she had wanted Lorimer to think of her differently, but all he did was stand there watching her laughing up at Charles with that hateful, contemptuous expression on his face and no doubt comparing her to Moira whose quiet composure might have been expressly designed to serve as an example of everything Skye was not. Next to her, Skye felt impossibly frivolous and out of place.

There was a tight feeling in her throat as if she wanted to burst into tears. Skye took desperate slugs of her wine and rattled off funny stories that kept Moira and her godparents amused but which only made Lorimer look even dourer. At first, Charles took her rather obvious attempts to flirt as his due, but as she got louder he began to look pained, obviously torn between his fear of offending his boss and his distrust of the frenetic edge in Skye's vivacity.

By the time they sat down to eat, Skye felt quite exhausted and decided to try being aloof and sophisticated again. She thought she was doing quite well, confusing everyone with her abrupt change of image, until one of Vanessa's earrings lost its precarious hold on her earlobes and fell with a loud splash into her soup, chinking against the fine china and splattering soup all over Charles who was sitting next to her. He looked vexed and dabbed irritably at his tie with his napkin while Skye bit her lip and stared down at the chunk of gold swimming in her soup in acute embarrassment. Why did these things always happen to her? Moira's earrings would never dare fall off.

There was an awkward silence, broken only by Charles's mutterings about his tie. Skye wanted to die. Fortunately, Marjorie intervened, glossing over the embarrassing moment with a comment to Moira and Skye risked a glance up. Lorimer was sitting opposite her, and he was making no attempt to help her out of her embarrassment by joining in the others' conversation and pretending nothing had happened. Instead he was watching her with a sort of resigned, reluctant amusement in his dark blue eyes. He shook his head at her, mouth twitching as an answering look of rueful laughter crept into Skye's expression and she fished the earring out of the soup with a fork.

Dipping a corner of her napkin into a glass of water, she wiped the earring clean and defiantly clipped it back on to her ear before meeting Lorimer's gaze once more, her eyes glinting with humour and challenge in the candlelight. For a long moment the others were forgotten as they looked at each across the table, before Lorimer, who had obviously been trying not to, gave in and grinned. Unable to help herself, Skye smiled back.

Then the moment was broken as Fleming recalled Lorimer's attention and Marjorie asked Skye if she wanted to finish her soup. Skye felt strangely lightheaded. Lorimer's smile had lit a slow-burning fuse inside her; she could feel its warmth spreading through her, trickling along her veins and tingling down to her fingertips. Somehow she carried on a conversation with Marjorie, but Lorimer kept catching insistently at her attention and she was very aware of his fingers curling round his wine glass, and the way he turned his head to smile at Moira. Every time he did that, Skye hurt inside. They were so obviously close to each other.

He didn't smile at her again. Slowly, the tingling warmth receded and Skye's smile grew increasingly brittle but she was determined to prove to Lorimer that while he might choose to ignore her others at least appreciated her company. She positively scintillated, dominating the conversation and sending Charles flirtatious glances under her lashes while a muscle began to beat insistently in Lorimer's rigid jaw.

Her bare shoulders gleamed softly as she leant forward eagerly, her face vivid even in the candlelight which threw haunting shadows into the hollows of collarbone and cleavage, and caught the glint of gold at her ears and in the shining hair piled on top of her head. It was slowly falling out of its neat arrangement, but since there was little point in pretending to be mysterious after your earring had dropped in the soup Skye pulled the combs free without thinking and shook her head so that her curls tumbled down in a pale, glinting mass. Still talking, she tossed her hair away from her face but, looking up, caught such a blaze of expression in Lorimer's eyes that she faltered. He turned away as soon as he saw her looking at him, and after only a moment's hesitation she struggled on with her story, but she was unnerved by her own reactions. Lorimer had no right to ignore her completely and then throw her into complete confusion with just a look!

She concentrated harder on Charles when they moved back into the sitting-room for coffee, but all the time she was aware of Lorimer who was looking more and more boot-faced. She didn't know why *he* was looking so cross; he was the one ignoring *her*, after all. What was she expected to do? Sit around and wait for him to smile at her again? Defiantly, she held out her glass to be refilled.

Skye had reached the buoyant stage and was inclined to protest when Lorimer stood up quite suddenly and announced that he would take her home.

'I can get a taxi!'

'I'm going in your direction anyway,' he said, his temper obviously on a short rein.

'What about Moira? And Charles?'

'If you'd been listening to someone other than yourself, you'd have heard us just discussing that, as Moira and Charles both live near by, he has kindly offered to walk her home. That leaves me in a car and you in no state to wander around on your own.'

Skye could see Fleming smothering a smile and she looked up at Lorimer indignantly and somewhat owlishly. 'I'm perfectly all right!'

'Don't argue, Skye.' Still protesting, she found herself being frog-marched down the steps and out to Lorimer's car, having been barely allowed enough time to kiss Fleming and Marjorie goodbye. Skye did notice that both of them wore very knowing smiles as they waved her off, but she was too taken up with Lorimer to wonder why.

'I would have been quite happy in a taxi,' she said sulkily as he got into the driver's seat.

Lorimer ignored her. 'Do up your seatbelt,' he ordered, starting the engine and glancing in the rear-view mirror before he pulled out. The orange glow of the street-lamp threw the decisive lines of his face into sharp relief so that he seemed to be blocked into angles of darkness and subdued light.

Skye obeyed him, still grumbling. 'You may have wanted to leave, but I was enjoying myself,' she said as she adjusted the seatbelt over her bare shoulder.

'You were the only one who was. I thought it was only fair to everyone else to stop you making an exhibition of yourself.' Lorimer's expression was sardonic as he glanced at her. She had unclipped her earrings with a sigh of relief and was massaging her sore earlobes. The mass of pale gold hair shimmered in the passing headlights.

'I was not making an exhibition of myself!' she said crossly. The defiant exhilaration that had kept her sparkling all evening was rapidly evaporating with only Lorimer as a very unresponsive audience. 'You know your trouble? You're so priggish and repressed, you don't know *how* to enjoy yourself!'

'What was there to enjoy in the spectacle of you making a fool of yourself over Charles Ferrars?' he retorted. '*He* certainly wasn't enjoying it either. I almost found it in myself to be sorry for him. God knows how Moira could think that you were fun! I thought you were appalling, and so did Ferrars.'

'How do you know what he thought?' said Skye rudely. 'You hardly said a word to him all evening.'

'You were talking so much, nobody got a word in to anyone! And anyway, I didn't have to talk to him to know that he was hating every minute of it. You might as well give up on him, Skye. You're much too loud and obvious to fit in with his smooth, careful image.'

'When I want your advice, I'll ask for it!' Skye shoved the earrings in her clutch-bag and snapped it shut angrily, turning her head deliberately away and preserving a silence that she hoped was dignified but which was more probably sullen. The car was juddering over the cobbles, each street-light surrounded by a fuzzy orange halo through the drifting mist. At least Skye told herself it was the mist blurring them rather than the tears that glistened unshed in her eyes.

Lorimer pulled the car up across the road from the flat. Skye stared up at the building. All the windows were dark, curtains closed against the cold night. She hoped the lights in the stairwell were working. They operated on a timer that had a nasty habit of stranding her halfway up to the fourth floor so that she had to grope for the next switch, and Skye had her own reasons for dreading the sudden plunge into pitch-darkness.

Unaware of the apprehensive look on her face, she was surprised when Lorimer offered abruptly, almost reluctantly, to see her safely inside. 'Would you?' she said gratefully, forgetting her sulks in her relief at not having to face that first blackness alone.

Without answering, he switched off the engine and walked with her across the road. Skye opened the heavy door and groped along the wall for the light switch. The stairwell sprung into dim light and she let out a sigh of relief.

'The light's working, thank goodness.' She glanced at Lorimer, feeling as always vaguely ashamed of her fear. 'It's stupid, I know, but when the lights go off it's pitch-black in here and I hate the thought of being alone in the dark.'

Lorimer's expression was unreadable. 'I don't suppose you were planning to be alone, were you?' He took a step towards her and for some reason Skye found herself retreating until she came up against the wall.

'Wh-what do you mean?' she stammered, her nerves jangling at his nearness. In the dim hall light, the impact of his hard presence was overwhelming and everything about him seemed to stand out in almost shocking detail: the grooves in his cheeks, the creases at the edge of his eyes, the way his hair grew, the cool, exciting line of his mouth.

'Come on, Skye,' he said with dangerous softness. 'You thought you'd be bringing Charles home with you tonight, but he wouldn't play, would he? It must be very disappointing for you, especially since you went to so much effort for him.'

Very deliberately, he reached out and brushed his finger along the line of her clavicle, a glancing, feather-light touch that scorched Skye's skin and set her senses thrumming. His body was blocking out the light, and her eyes gleamed through the shadows. She couldn't breathe; each shallow gasp took an enormous effort and when Lorimer traced a thoughtful line down to the shadowy hollow of her cleavage she thought her heart would stop altogether.

She wanted to jerk herself away from the wall, to push his hand away and march up the stairs with her head held high, but his eyes held her immobile as treacherous, insidious desire coiled itself round her will. Lorimer was barely touching her, but she knew he could feel her skin quivering in response.

'You looked beautiful tonight,' he said and his voice was deep and grudging. 'It would be a shame to waste all that effort, don't you think?' Both his hands were sliding tantalisingly over her bare shoulders, his fingers warm and very strong against her satiny skin, drifting inevitably up her throat to slide beneath the soft, tangled hair. 'Don't you think so?' he asked again, very softly.

Skye couldn't have answered even if she had wanted to. She was beyond speaking, beyond thinking, every sense snarled in a helpless tangle of temptation, and then it was too late anyway, as he bent his head and kissed her.

The touch of his lips was a spark to dry tinder; Skye knew intuitively that he was as unprepared as she for the flame of response that leapt between them. Perhaps, too, he was as helpless to control its searing power, for after that one shocked moment his hands tightened in her hair and his kiss deepened as he pushed her back against the wall.

Skye was lost, abandoned to sheer sensation. Her hands had gone up in instinctive defence but instead of pushing Lorimer away as a faint, still sensible voice told her to they tightened around the lapels of his dinner-jacket, and she kissed him back with a kind of desperation. Caught up in the same breathless spiral of desire, his mouth moved hungrily against hers, and his hands slid from her throat to pull her harder against him.

Skye was molten in his arms, careless now of everything but the need burning through her. She couldn't kiss him deep enough, hold him close enough. She felt as if she was dissolving in the spinning excitement of his mouth on hers, his hard hands moving possessively over her body. Fumbling with the buttons, she undid his jacket and slid her arms around him, thrilling at the steely strength of his body.

Gasping for breath between kisses, they clung together, oblivious to the fact that the stair light had switched itself off automatically. Skye had not known what it was to *feel* so intensely. She was dizzy with longing, intoxicated with an increasingly urgent need, and when his mouth left hers she arched her throat so that he could blizzard frenzied kisses down and along her shoulders, muttering her name almost accusingly.

His fingers were groping for the zip at the back of her dress as she tugged his shirt free at last and let her hands drift luxuriously over his back with a murmur of pleasure. His skin was warm and sleek, and she felt his muscles flex at her touch even as her own spine shuddered in response to the demand of his hands.

'God, Skye...' At first Skye didn't realise that Lorimer had dragged himself back to reality. Her lips were against the pulse thundering below his ear, her tongue exploring the taste and texture of his skin when he buried his face in her hair. Only gradually did she realise that his hands had stilled and that his back was rigid as he fought to bring his breathing back under control. Very slowly, he drew the zip back up and let his hands drop as he lifted his head. Then he reached along the wall and switched on the light again.

Skye felt as if she had been dropped without warning into a pool of icy water. The light which had seemed so dim before was suddenly harsh, cruelly illuminating her bruised, trembling mouth and dishevelled hair. Her eyes were huge and still dazed with desire as she collapsed back against the wall, her knees trembling so much that she was terribly afraid she would just slide to the floor at Lorimer's feet.

For a long moment they just stared at each other as if unable to believe what had happened between them. Somewhere outside, a car changed gear and a siren wailed, but inside the damp, musty hall there was only the sound of their ragged breathing, unnaturally loud in the silence.

'Charles is luckier than he knows,' said Lorimer at last with a twisted smile. 'If he'd come back with you tonight, he would never have been able to resist an invitation like that, and then he would have been well and truly in your toils, wouldn't he?'

Skye said nothing. Shivers of sensation were still rippling over her skin like aftershocks. She moistened her lips, but found that she was physically incapable of speaking so she just concentrated on clinging to the wall instead.

'Next time,' he went on when she didn't answer. 'I would forget about the jokes if I were you, Skye, and lure him straight to a dark room. I'm sure you'll have better success that way.'

Skye found her voice at last, or at least a pathetic imitation of it. 'Go away,' she whispered.

'Don't look so tragic,' Lorimer said harshly. 'I was just ensuring that all your best efforts at seduction didn't go entirely to waste.' He turned towards the door, then changed his mind. As if against his better judgement, he pulled her into his arms once more for one brief, hard kiss. 'Think of it as a practice run,' he suggested and let her go. At the door, he turned once more. 'I'll see you on Monday. Try to be on time for once.' Then the door swung shut behind him and he was gone.

'Anyway, darling, at least I don't have to worry about you,' her father concluded with determined cheerfulness. 'Fleming's been telling me about Lorimer Kingan. I gather he's keeping your nose to the grindstone, but that won't be doing you any harm. I can't tell you what a relief it is to know that you're in good hands for a change.'

Skye thought about Lorimer's hands, on her skin, in her hair, hard against her. She didn't think that was quite what her father meant, but he sounded so worried about his business problems that she didn't have the heart to tell him that Lorimer's hands were far from safe.

She had been devastated when Lorimer had left her last night. Shocked by the explosion of desire and still shaking from the abrupt return to reality, she had slumped back against the wall, squeezing her eyes shut against the memory of his kiss and the throb of unsatisfied need, until the light had clicked off again and she had had to fumble for the switch.

She had been determined then never to see Lorimer again. Her face burned when she remembered how she had clung to him, her kisses deep and desperate and her hands urgent over the hard, compact, exciting strength of his back, heedless of anything but the touch and the taste and the feel of him. How could she have been so uncontrolled? She would never be able to face him again, not knowing that he too would remember.

Her father was reminding her jovially of all the times he had fretted over the way she had drifted from unsuitable job to unsuitable job, and Skye realised for the first time just how thoughtless she had been. It was the first time, too, that her father had ever mentioned his own problems to her. Why should he always be the one to do the worrying? she thought, suddenly ashamed. He had always been there for her, helping her out of the messes she inevitably got herself into without question, and now it was her turn to do something for him. All he wanted was for her to stick with this job to the end of the three months. It wasn't much to ask, and Skye didn't have it in her to tell him, now that he was so pleased for her, that she had decided to chuck in yet another job. Another mess, another failure. Couldn't she do *anything* right?

Would it be so hard to carry on working for Lorimer? Skye asked herself. It wasn't as if it would happen again. Lorimer wasn't interested in her. That kiss had been ... well, what had it been? A challenge? A punishment? A means of venting his irritation with her? It hadn't had anything to do with love. And his casual words as he had left her shattered had shown more clearly than anything that the whole episode had left him unmoved.

Well, if he could treat it like that, so could she. Welcome anger flickered along Skye's veins, warming her out of her numb sense of despair, and if her father had been able to see her his brows would have lifted at the suddenly defiant tilt of her chin. Lorimer had no business kissing her like that anyway! Nor need he think that she would give up her job because of one crummy kiss. She would go into the office on Monday as normal, and she would behave as if absolutely nothing had happened. Nothing really *had* happened. It was just a kiss, that was all.

That was all.

CHAPTER SIX

'HAVE you got anything planned with Charles this week?'

Skye looked up warily from her word processor as Lorimer came into her office one Wednesday. Over the last two weeks, she had schooled herself to appear cool and unconcerned, but she still couldn't prevent the jump of her heart whenever he appeared. Lorimer himself had made no reference to the kisses they had shared and behaved so exactly as he had done before that sometimes Skye wondered if she had imagined it. Once or twice, she caught him watching her unawares, but his expression was always inscrutable and she could only hope that her own betrayed nothing of the memories that still tormented her.

The atmosphere between them was strained and snappy, much as it always had been, and as it became obvious that Lorimer was not going to mention the kiss Skye gradually relaxed. She was still careful not to touch him, but she deliberately gave herself no time to think, and remember. At work, she dragged Sheila out to lunch or bullied the others into going out in the evenings, and the rest of the time galvanised Vanessa and her friends into a whirlwind of activity. Vanessa complained that she was exhausted, but Skye's inexhaustible energy was fuelled by a dogged determination not to let Lorimer guess for one minute that she had given his kisses another thought.

'What if I have?' she asked suspiciously now. She hadn't heard a word from Charles since that fateful night, but she didn't want Lorimer to know that.

'You'll have to cancel, if you have,' he said brusquely. 'You're coming down to Galloway with me tomorrow and we'll be staying there until the weekend.'

'Thanks for the notice!'

Lorimer scowled at her sarcasm. 'In case you hadn't noticed, this is an office, not a dating agency. I can't make all my arrangements to suit you.' He dropped a file into her in tray. 'We'll stay at the Kielven Inn; give them a ring and let them know we'll be arriving tomorrow afternoon.'

'What if they're full?'

'At the end of the November? We'll have the place to ourselves. I stay there often, anyway, so there won't be a problem. Now, we've been invited to lunch with the Buchanans on the way down. They own the house I want to turn into the hotel at the heart of the new complex, and I've finally managed to talk them into renegotiating after the fiasco with the English investors. Nothing's been finally agreed, though, so it's vital that you give the right impression of the company. That means you're to keep quiet, behave yourself and for God's sake try and look a little more businesslike and a little less like a liquorice allsort!' He averted his eyes from her boldly patterned jumper and striped leggings. 'I'll pick you up at nine o'clock tomorrow morning. Please be ready and waiting outside your flat, as I've no intention of finding somewhere to park at that time of morning and climbing up four flights of stairs to find out what's happened to you.'

Inevitably, Skye overslept. She had spent a wild night out with Vanessa's crowd, trying to persuade herself that if any one of the young men there kissed her as Lorimer had done it would have just the same effect. Only she'd known that it wouldn't. They were friendly and fun, but none of them had Lorimer's mouth or Lorimer's hands or Lorimer's hard, strong body.

At nine o'clock on the dot, a car horn blasted impatiently below the flat, and Skye, who had fallen out of bed only twenty minutes before, hung precariously out of the window, hair still wet from a rapid shower, and waved to catch Lorimer's attention.

She could see him frown and get out of the car, looking pointedly at his watch. 'Can you give me ten minutes?' she yelled down at him, so that everyone in the street stopped and craned their necks up to see what was going on.

Lorimer stiffened with annoyance at finding himself part of a public spectacle. He pointed at his car, double-parked with the engine running. 'One minute,' he shouted back. 'If you're not here by then, I'm going without you and you can start looking for another job.'

Grumbling, Skye threw her hairdrier into the suitcase banged it shut and grabbed her make-up from the bathroom. With no time to think, she had simply grabbed everything out of her wardrobe and shoved it into the case, with the result that it was far too heavy and she had to bump it down the stairs.

She was pink-cheeked and breathless by the time she erupted out on to the pavement, trailing her jacket and scarf and trying to fix in her earrings—she had opted for zebras today—while still struggling to keep her make-up bag wedged under her arm.

Lorimer got out of the car wearing an expression of profound irritation and took the suitcase from her.

'What on earth have you got in here?' We're only going away for a couple of nights!'

'I wasn't sure what I'd need,' Skye gasped, having finally managed to hook in the second earring. 'So I brought everything.' She got into the car and collapsed back into her seat, fanning herself with her diary.

'I hope "everything" includes something more sensible than what you've got on now,' said Lorimer, wincing visibly as he took in the full glory of Skye's outfit. Skye herself had been rather pleased with her choice. She thought it was rather smart, but Lorimer obviously had other ideas. He eyed her short skirt and belted top, both zebra-striped in black and white, then his gaze travelled down long, slim legs, encased in sheer black tights, to black high-heeled shoes. He sighed. 'I thought I told you to look businesslike?'

'What's wrong with this?' Skye gestured down at herself. 'This is smart! I chose it specially because it was black and white and you said you didn't want any bright colours.' She pushed back her hair and flicked her earrings at him. 'Look, I've even got these to match. I've never been so co-ordinated before!'

'We're going to Galloway, not the Masai Mara,' Lorimer pointed out caustically. 'The whole idea of this trip is for you to keep quiet and fade into the background. I'm supposed to be persuading the Buchanans that this is a reputable development that will prove an asset to the local community, and they're unlikely to be convinced when I turn up with a secretary who looks as if she's just off on safari.' He cast her an irritable glance as he waited to turn out on to Bruntsfield Place. 'Don't you possess anything *plain*?'

Skye ran a mental eye over her wardrobe. 'Only my black dress,' she said without thinking, and then could have kicked herself. She had been so careful over the last fortnight to make no references to that evening. What had possessed her to mention the dress now? The very thought of it brought back haunting memories of that dim hallway and the breathless passion that had gripped them so unexpectedly. Did Lorimer remember the dress? Did he remember tracing its neckline with that one tantalising finger? Did he remember unzipping it slowly, easing it down over her shoulders?

Skye swallowed. She just wished she could forget. She slanted a look at his profile under her lashes. He was frowning at the traffic, drumming his fingers on the steering-wheel, but as if aware of her gaze he glanced across at her.

'Oh, *that* dress?' he said drily. Obviously he *did* remember. Skye wished she'd kept her mouth shut. She bit her lip and longed to be able to look cool and unconcerned. 'I hardly think a dress with that kind of inflammable effect would be very suitable for a trip like this either,' he went on, and a disquieting smile glinted in his eyes. 'You're the only girl I know that can dress in unrelieved black and still look gaudy!'

'What does it matter what I'm wearing anyway?' Skye said hastily, anxious to steer the conversation out of these dangerous waters. 'Nobody's going to notice me if I have to fade into the background and not say anything.'

'How can you fade into the background looking like that?' Lorimer demanded as he acknowledged a taxi driver who had stopped to let him pull across the traffic. 'I want people to listen to what I'm saying, not goggle at you.'

'But I won't say anything!'

'You won't need to say anything,' he said sourly. 'You'll just need to sit there with those legs.'

Skye looked down at her tights in case they were laddered. 'What's wrong with them?'

'There's nothing wrong with them. Far from it.' He glanced at her knees, and Skye, suddenly conscious of how her skirt rode up over her thighs when she sat down, gave the hem a surreptitious tug. 'They're just too...' He hesitated, searching for the right word. 'Distracting,' he decided at last.

'But I've often worn skirts this length in the office and you've never been distracted,' Skye pointed out huffily.

Lorimer concentrated on the traffic. 'Everything about you is distracting, Skye.'

At that time of morning, the roads were still busy with rush-hour traffic and their progress was slow. Skye watched the pedestrians walking along the sunny side of the street, heads bent against the brisk wind. What did he mean, 'distracting'? She wished he didn't have this ability to unsettle her. She wished she'd never mentioned that wretched dress. She wished she could forget how warm and exciting his mouth had been.

Perhaps she would feel better if she had had time to get ready this morning? Suddenly remembering her naked face, Skye fished her make-up out of her bag and began scrabbling in its depths for a mirror. A slick of mascara and a dash of lipstick, and she might feel readier to face the day.

'What *are* you doing?' Lorimer asked testily as they stopped at yet another red light.

'Looking for my mirror.'

'What on earth for?'

'I want do do my eyes ... oh, never mind, I'll use this instead.' Abandoning her search, Skye calmly twisted the rear-view mirror round to face her and unscrewed her mascara.

'What the——?' Lorimer cast her an incredulous look and grabbed it back. 'I'm driving!'

'You don't need it when we're stuck in traffic,' Skye pointed out reasonably and turned it back to her side. 'I won't be a minute.' Opening her blue eyes wide, she began carefully stroking on the mascara.

Lorimer gripped the top of the steering-wheel very tightly and rested his forehead on his hands. 'God give me strength!'

'Oh, don't make such a fuss!' Skye was still disgruntled by her rushed start. 'It's not that bad.' She pulled the top of her bright pink lipstick and twisted it up. 'I'm only putting on a bit of make-up. I know this is Morningside, but surely even here a bit of lipstick doesn't count as a cardinal sin?'

'Skye, you don't seem to realise that we're going to the country,' said Lorimer through his teeth. 'We're going to be tramping over muddy fields and negotiating with tough old farmers, not taking part in some fashion show. You're going to look out of place as it is, without going over the top with cosmetics.'

'Well, if I'm going to look that out of place, a dab of lipstick isn't going to make much difference, is it?' Skye said rather indistinctly as she blotted her lipstick carefully with a tissue. 'Besides, I feel better if I've got some on.' Lorimer stared at her in baffled frustration as she snapped the lid back on the lipstick, dropped it back in her bag and smiled brightly at him. 'It's green,' she said kindly, pointing at the traffic light.

The cars banked up behind them were already tooting their horns impatiently. 'You're so superficial,' said Lorimer, grinding the gears in his bad temper at having been caught unawares. 'You don't seem to think of anything but your appearance. 'I shall be glad when Moira takes over from you and I can have a secretary who's capable of thinking about something other than herself for a change.'

'Moira was wearing make-up at Fleming's,' Skye said, nettled. 'I didn't notice you giving *her* a lecture about being superficial!'

'Moira wasn't at work. You are. This isn't just a jaunt into the countryside, Skye. It's taken me a long time to set up this deal and I don't want you jeopardising all my negotiations with some flippant remark. It'll be bad enough taking another English girl down as it is. God knows what the Buchanans will think when they clap eyes on you!'

'Honestly, anyone would think I were some kind of alien!'

'An alien might be a little more predictable than you seem to be. As far as I can see, your approach to life is completely illogical.'

'We can't all be programmed to think like computers,' Skye protested. 'Millions of people are illogical. It doesn't make us freaks.'

They had been inching along behind a double-decker bus, but Lorimer managed to overtake it at last. 'You can't tell me millions of people would drop everything to follow a man who was patently uninterested in them!'

Skye flushed. 'Who says Charles isn't interested in me?'

'Is he?'

There was a short silence. Skye looked out of the window at the solid Edinburgh houses with their austere façades that gave little hint of the warmth and comfort within. Like Lorimer, she thought irrelevantly, with his stern mouth and his forbidding frown and his ability to turn her emotions upside-down with the merest touch. How could she tell him that she hadn't given Charles a thought since that devastating kiss?

'I haven't given up hope,' she said stiffly. Let Lorimer think that she was still hooked on Charles. She had few enough defences against him as it was; she couldn't let her pride crumble too.

'Ever obsessed,' Lorimer sneered. 'I can't think what you see in him. He seems a cold fish to me.'

'That's good coming from you!'

'What makes you think I'm cold, Skye?' Lorimer cast a brief sideways glance at her averted profile as they reached the dual carriageway and he accelerated out of the traffic. 'Did you think I was cold when I kissed you?'

Skye felt a humiliating wave of colour sweep up her throat to stain her cheeks scarlet. 'I would have thought you'd want to forget that particular episode,' she managed with difficulty at last.

'Would you?' he said unhelpfully, and in spite of herself Skye's eyes flickered across to meet his. His expression was quite unreadable.

'Well, *I* want to forget about it,' she said, as if to convince herself.

'Why? You enjoyed it . . . and don't try and deny it,' he added as Skye opened her mouth to try and deny it.

'Why should I enjoy being kissed by you when I'm in love with Charles?' she asked, stung by the cool mockery in his voice.

'Perhaps it means you're not in love with him at all.'

'I hope you're not suggesting I'm in love with *you*?' said Skye furiously.

'I hardly think that's likely,' said Lorimer with another cool look. 'It certainly won't get you very far if you are!

You need to find a long-suffering type who's prepared to put up with you.'

'I don't *need* anybody.' Skye didn't know whether she felt more hurt or angry. 'I'm perfectly happy on my own.'

'No one would guess it from the way you carry on. You pursue Charles Ferrars four hundred miles, and then when he gives you no encouragement you start on my staff.'

'Your...?' Skye gaped at him, astonishment momentarily conquering her anger. 'What are you talking about?'

'I've seen you chatting up every male in the office. You're all smiles and laughs and fluttering eyelashes with *them*.' A sudden suspicion that the strange note in his voice was jealousy flashed through Skye's mind, only to be instantly dismissed. He would never have been able to mock the suggestion that she might be in love with him if he was jealous. He could hardly have made it clearer that the very idea appalled him.

'I do *not* flutter my eyelashes,' she said crossly. 'I'm just being friendly.'

'What about all these invitations to go out in the evening? I suppose an office doesn't give you enough scope! You always seem to be going out with someone or other.'

Skye was surprised that he had even noticed. 'Haven't you ever heard of a social life?'

'I just don't want you upsetting anyone. They were all quite happy before, but you've stirred them all up. Girls like you always mean trouble. Next thing, I'll have all my men at each other's throats over your big blue eyes!'

The big blue eyes in question were flashing dangerously. 'The occasional trip to the pub is hardly likely to *upset* anyone! You just don't like the idea of your staff enjoying themselves.'

'Don't be ridiculous,' he snapped. 'The only thing I don't like is the sight of a woman going all out to get a man.'

Skye gave an exasperated sigh. She wished she had never told Lorimer about her crush on Charles. 'I'm surprised you could bear to bring me along with you on this trip,' she said sarcastically. 'Aren't you afraid I'll jump on the first man I meet?'

'You're not likely to have much success on *this* trip,' said Lorimer. 'You'll remind people too much of Caroline.'

'Caroline?'

'She was the executive sent up from London by my original investors. I brought her down to Galloway to look at the site, but she managed to upset the Buchanans and alienate Duncan McPherson so completely that the whole deal fell through. The Buchanans have come round, but Duncan's a stubborn old devil and he's not likely to forgive the way Caroline treated him. I'm going to have to approach him very carefully. He owns the farm adjoining the Buchanans' property and some of his fields which have been set aside because of over-production would be perfect for another nine holes of the golf course. I'm keen to get hold of his land as an eighteen-hole course is essential for the sort of prestige development we're aiming for, but Duncan won't discuss anything on the phone, so I'm going to try and beard him in his den tomorrow. Whether he'll be prepared to listen or not is another matter.'

'What happens if he won't?'

'We *could* go ahead without him and have a nine-hole course, but I want this hotel to be up with the best, and that means eighteen holes.'

'So if you can't get this Duncan McPherson to agree to sell you his set-aside land, you might have to abandon the whole idea?'

'That's about it.' Lorimer grimaced. 'I'm convinced that I can turn the Buchanans' house and grounds into a superb hotel and golf course, but it's a question of getting all the different parties to agree. I'm so close to putting all the pieces together after Caroline's disastrous intervention, but if I lose one bit, like Duncan McPherson's land, the rest will fall apart again, and with it my reputation.' His brows were drawn together in concentration as he considered the problem. 'I've spent years working my way to the top of the market, and changing direction like this means putting my reputation—and that of my firm—on the line, but it's more than that in this case. Galloway is an area that means a lot to me. Making a success of this development is important to me personally as well as professionally, hence my reluctance to have you as my PA. I don't want to risk offending anybody by giving them the idea that I've got another Caroline in tow.'

'Am I so like her?' Skye asked, not at all sure that she wanted to know the answer.

'You're English,' he said as if that was all that mattered. 'That'll probably be enough to tar you with the same brush, but otherwise no, you're not like her at all. Caroline was very smart, very efficient, very arrogant and utterly ruthless. She didn't care whom she trampled on to get her own way.' Lorimer's voice was tinged with bitterness and Skye glanced at him. Had he been attracted to Caroline only to find himself disillusioned? It seemed unlikely; Lorimer wasn't the kind of man who got trampled on. Still, it might explain his resentment of the English.

'Was she attractive?'

Lorimer shrugged. 'Very, if you like ice queens.'

'She sounds just your type,' said Skye grumpily. 'Cool, smart, efficient... all the qualities you're always complaining that I haven't got.'

'There's a difference between efficiency and being hard as nails.' Skye decided she had been wrong about the bitterness. Now he simply sounded bad-tempered. 'You and Caroline are at two different extremes. She was ruthless, you're hopeless, but when it comes to the kind of girl I would least like to have at my side on this trip it's hard to choose between you. Frankly, I'd have preferred to have left you in Edinburgh, but I don't see why I should pay you to sit around on your hands when I need an assistant down here.' He glanced across at Skye. 'I just hope you've realised how important it is for you to keep quiet and let me do the talking.'

Skye folded her hands virtuously and assumed a lofty expression. 'You won't even know I'm there,' she promised and Lorimer sighed.

'I'll believe that when I see it!'

They drove past the source of the Tweed and on through bare yellow-brown hills. Skye spotted the occasional isolated farmhouse but otherwise the landscape was empty except for a scattering of resigned-looking sheep and the pine plantations slowly spreading dark green tentacles over the bleak grandeur. It all looked deceptively mellow in the pale sunshine, but she shivered as they passed the Devil's Beef Tub, a huge, natural hollow in the hills where the Border thieves used to hide their stolen cattle and where the Devil reputedly laughed as he threw his victims from the top. Even on a bright day like this, the place had a brooding, sinister atmosphere, and she was glad that Lorimer didn't stop the car.

Once down from the hills, the country was softer and more gentle. Trees lined the winding roads and the famous Belted Galloways with their wide white bands around their middles grazed contentedly in the fields. There was something so still and timeless in the way they stood, heads down, legs staggered, their black and white colouring striking against the Galloway green grass that Skye couldn't help remembering the plastic cows on the toy farm her brothers had had when they were small.

They reached Glendorie at midday. The Buchanans lived in a great grey granite house outside the little village, and Skye could see instantly what a wonderful setting it would be for a hotel. The low hills behind rolled down into woodland, and the lawn in front of the house stretched down to the water which was too big to be a mere burn, too small to merit being called a river, although it was flowing high and fast today.

The Buchanans were a gentle couple in their late seventies, obviously rattling around in the huge house. They came out of the house as the car crunched over the gravel, accompanied by two black Labradors.

'Now, remember, you're to behave yourself,' Lorimer reminded Skye as she reached for the door-handle. 'And please don't drink too much. We don't want another performance like the one you gave at Fleming's!'

'Don't worry,' Skye flashed back with a challenging look. 'I wouldn't risk a repetition of what happened afterwards!' Pinning a bright smile on her face, she got out of the car before he had a chance to reply.

She was determined to show Lorimer that she was more than capable of appearing quietly aloof, but her impression of dignified reserve was immediately ruined by the two Labradors who bustled up excitedly to greet her. Ignoring Angus Buchanan's embarrassed attempt to call them off, they thrust their heads under her hand until she laughed and patted their sleek coats.

'Oh, dear, you'll be covered in dog hairs now,' said Isobel Buchanan apologetically as she pushed the dogs aside and shook Skye's hand. 'I hope you don't mind the dogs?'

'Of course not.' Skye smiled at her, warm and friendly and transparently honest. 'We always had Labradors at home. They're lovely dogs, aren't they?'

'They obviously like *you*, anyway.' Angus Buchanan turned from greeting Lorimer to eye Skye with undisguised approval. 'Always a good judge of character, dogs.'

'As long as they haven't ruined that smart outfit.' His wife had been studying her guest's striking appearance with some alarm, but was evidently relieved when Skye only laughed.

'Lorimer would say it just served me right if they had,' she confessed. 'He wanted me to wear a twin set and pearls or some scratchy tweed.'

Reassured, Mrs Buchanan smiled back. 'There's plenty of time for twin sets and tweeds when you get older. I like to see young people dressing with a bit of style.'

Skye was unable to resist shooting Lorimer a look of triumph. 'You're supposed to be fading into the background,' he hissed in her ear as they went into the comfortable sitting-room.

Skye tried. She really tried, but the Buchanans had evidently decided to trust their dogs' judgement and plied her with questions. Before long, Skye was chatting happily away, a sedate glass of sherry in her hand, fondling the Labradors' ears as she admired photographs of the Buchanan grandchildren in Australia.

'Another sherry, Skye?'

Angus Buchanan was standing over her, beaming. Behind him, Lorimer sent her a minatory look which Skye had no difficulty in interpreting as an order to refuse politely and shut up. Meeting his gaze with a bland smile, she held out her glass. 'How lovely! Thank you!'

She was in sparkling form over lunch, and the Buchanans were clearly delighted with her. Lorimer, unable to shout at her as he was undoubtedly longing to do, sat looking increasingly boot-faced and seized the first opportunity after coffee to drag her out of the room.

'Would you mind if I took Skye with me to look round the house? I'd like to take a few measurements.'

'Of course, of course.' Angus clapped him on the shoulder. 'Enjoying ourselves so much, we'd forgotten you were here on business! You must forget yourself with a delightful assistant like Skye around! No, you carry on. Go wherever you like.'

'Skye?' Lorimer stood impatiently at the door and spoke her name through clenched teeth but Skye, with two sherries and a glass of wine under her belt, only finished her coffee with an infuriating lack of haste.

She put down her cup and got to her feet with a wink at Angus. 'Coming, oh, master!'

All the way up the grand staircase she had to listen to the furious tirade that Lorimer had been bottling up over lunch. She was an appalling exhibitionist. Why couldn't she ever do what she was told? She had deliberately set out to make him look ridiculous. She was flippant, unbusinesslike, thoroughly untrustworthy, absolutely impossible.

Suspecting that he was merely cross that he had been proved so wrong about the Buchanans hating her just because she was English, Skye bore it patiently and waited until he had got it all out of his system. Sure enough, when they reached the top of the stairs, Lorimer stopped as if he had abruptly run out of steam and looked down at her.

Quite unperturbed by his savage denunciation of her character, Skye wisely said nothing but merely gave him a sunny smile, her eyes a bright, guileless blue. Lorimer struggled, but in the end even he wasn't proof against their dancing appeal. 'You're hopeless,' he said with a sudden, exasperated grin, and took her arm to lead her down the corridor.

Strangely enough, Lorimer's tirade had cleared the air, and Skye felt unaccountably light-hearted as he showed her round the house. Upstairs, the rooms were in a poor state of repair and most of Lorimer's notes were to do with the immediate alterations and restoration that would be necessary. The Buchanans had admitted over lunch that the maintenance of the house had become too much for them to cope with. Both their children were living overseas, and much as they had loved it the house was now a burden they were anxious to get rid of, as long as there were no more of the complications that had upset them so much before.

'The property ends at the burn there.' Lorimer was standing in the embrasure of a bedroom window and Skye joined him there to peer in the direction of his pointing finger. 'Duncan McPherson's land lies on the other side. You can see what a difference it would make if that were to be included in the complex. The first tee would be over there and the course would go up and around the side——' he gestured '—and end up back here at the eighteenth green. It could be a first-class course if I can only persuade Duncan to sell.'

Skye looked rather doubtfully over the water. 'What if he just doesn't *want* to sell his land?'

'He got as far as considering the idea before Caroline threw a spanner in the works, so I don't think it's got any particular sentimental value. The fields aren't worth much as they are, and frankly Duncan could probably do with the money, but you'd never get him to admit as much.'

'We all have our pride,' Skye pointed out.

'Even you?'

They were turning back to the room together and suddenly found each other very close, far closer than they had let themselves be over the last two weeks. Their eyes met and held.

Skye felt the breath dry in her throat and her heart began to thump slowly, painfully. The memory of his kiss was suddenly so vivid that she could almost feel his mouth against hers, his hands tracing patterns of fire down her spine. She could taste his lips and smell the warm, clean, masculine scent of his skin. Her fingertips tingled as if she could still feel his hard muscles beneath her hands.

He was only inches away. Half a step away and she could touch him, slide her arms around him, raise her lips to his and beg him to kiss her again . . . Skye dragged her wildly careering thoughts to a halt. She didn't need to take that step to know what Lorimer's reaction would be. Pride, she reminded herself. That was all she had.

Swallowing, she forced her eyes away from his and stepped back into the safety of the wide room. Her voice was so husky that she had to clear her throat. 'Even me,' she said.

CHAPTER SEVEN

Angus Buchanan was waiting for them at the bottom of the stairs. 'Everything all right?'

'Yes, fine.' Lorimer seemed to shake himself free of the strain that had sprung up as he and Skye had stood by the window and looked into each other's eyes. 'The only problem is likely to be Duncan McPherson, as you know, Angus. If he refuses to sell, well, it might affect my investor's decision.'

Angus Buchanan looked troubled. 'I doubt you'll get very far with Duncan. He was never keen on the idea of a hotel here at the best of times, and after the business with that woman...' He heaved his big shoulders. 'Well, he's downright hostile. You'll be lucky to see him at all.'

'I'll see what I can do tomorrow,' Lorimer promised. 'Don't worry yet. If the worst comes to the worst, I'll try to raise the capital somewhere else again. I can always sell the manse.'

'You can't do that!' Isobel Buchanan sounded shocked. 'It's such a lovely house and it so badly needs to be looked after. I do think it's a shame it was allowed to fall into such a state—although anyone looking at this house might say the same about us!'

'You can tell this house has been loved, though,' said Skye, wondering what manse they were talking about. 'It's full of happy memories, even a casual visitor can sense that. That's what makes it so welcoming.'

Isobel looked approvingly at her. 'Quite right, dear, I always feel that a house needs children and laughter.

117

The manse is crying out for a family to live in it.' She turned teasingly to Lorimer. 'I hope you heard that, Lorimer! It's high time you were married.'

Skye was shocked at the coldness that gripped her heart. The Buchanans had obviously known Lorimer for some time and if they thought he was going to get married...

'I don't have any plans at present,' said Lorimer, carefully expressionless.

'Oh, I'm sorry...' Mrs Buchanan broke off in confusion and looked from him to Skye and back again. 'I thought...'

Skye felt a blush steal up her cheeks. 'I'm just a secretary,' she said hastily at the same time as Lorimer said,

'Skye's just helping me out until Moira Lindsay's free to start work. You know Moira, don't you?'

'Er, yes, of course.' Isobel was obviously mortified by her *faux pas*. 'Such a nice girl.'

There was an awkward pause as they all walked out to the car. 'Are you going to the presentation dinner on Saturday night?' Angus asked Lorimer to fill the silence. 'You're a member, aren't you? And if you're staying at the Kielven Inn, you'll be right on the spot. You can't do better than the local golf club's annual thrash when it comes to making local contacts—and believe me you're going to need them if you want to make a success of this hotel idea.'

Lorimer hesitated, glancing at Skye. 'Would you mind staying another day?'

'Of course she wouldn't!' said Angus heartily before she had a chance to reply. 'She looks like the kind of girl who'd enjoy a party. I'll make sure there are a couple of tickets for you at the door.'

'I'm sorry about that,' Lorimer apologised to Skye as they drove off. 'I can put you on a train if you'd rather go back to Edinburgh tomorrow night.'

'I don't mind staying.' They were being very polite to each other, very strained. The winter afternoon was closing in rapidly, and the headlights cast a blurry beam through the dark blue mist. 'I didn't realise that you knew the Buchanans so well.'

'I don't know them very well, but I grew up not far from here, so I remember them, of course. They were very kind when...' Lorimer broke off abruptly. 'When my father died,' he finished after a tiny pause, but Skye had the feeling that that hadn't been what he was originally going to say. His face was closed and there was a note in his voice that warned her not to ask any more.

'What's this manse they were talking about?' she asked instead.

'It's an old house down by the coast,' he said, and she sensed he was relieved at the change of subject. 'I hadn't been back for years, but I was driving around one day last year, looking for a suitable site for the hotel, and I found it at the end of a road.' He paused, remembering how he had first seen the manse, and unconsciously his face softened. 'It was practically a ruin, and not nearly big enough for a hotel, but I suppose you could say that I fell in love with it. The builders have been in all summer, and it should be weatherproof by now. In fact, I'd like to go over and check what they've done if we have time.'

'What's it like?' said Skye, enjoying the unguarded look on his face when he talked about his house.

'It's right by the sea,' he said, 'and it looks across the estuary at the hills. It's all sea and sky and light.' He shrugged, half embarrassed by his eloquence. 'It's also far too big and quite impractical. Isobel's right. It needs a family.'

Skye looked out of the window and concentrated on keeping her voice light. 'You might have a family one day.'

There was a short silence. 'I don't think so,' said Lorimer flatly. 'Marriage and a family are for people who believe in happy endings.'

'And you don't?' she asked, shocked by the cynicism in his voice.

'No,' he said. 'I don't.'

Lorimer parked the car off the track beneath an old oak tree. 'I'll walk the rest of the way,' he said from the back, pulling on a pair of old gumboots. 'You heard what Angus Buchanan said about Duncan. He's still feeling bitter, so it's best if he doesn't see you at all. You stay here and wait till I come back.' He shut the boot and walked round the car to tap on her window. Skye unwound it with an enquiring look. 'Please don't wander off or do anything stupid,' he said.

'I don't see how I can do anything stupid stuck in a car,' she grumbled.

'Nor do I, but I wouldn't put anything past you.'

Sulking, she watched his tall, massive figure stride up the track and out of sight. The car seemed very empty without him.

Last night had been awkward. As Lorimer had predicted, they were the only guests at the Kielven Inn, and they had eaten in an empty, echoing dining-room, desperately making polite conversation to disguise the tension that was still strumming in the air between them. In the end, Skye had pleaded a tiredness she didn't in the least feel and had escaped to her room. She had lain on her bed listening to the sounds of cheerful chatter from the bar below and wondered why Lorimer was so bitter about marriage. His warning, if that was what it had been, had only seemed to exacerbate the strained atmosphere between them. There had always been a snappy edge to their relationship, of course, but this was different. The snappiness had disappeared and in its lace was an unease, a feeling of disquiet that Skye couldn't identify and that had intensified over dinner as they found themselves picking their words with as much care as if they had been making their way over a minefield.

Staring up at the ceiling, she tried to work out just what had changed, and when, and why. *Something* had happened as they looked at each other by that bedroom window, but just what it was she couldn't decide. All she knew was that it was much easier when Lorimer was being disagreeable. Anything was better than this strained awareness.

She had changed her mind the next morning when Lorimer had insisted on taking her to the Kielven golf course to introduce her to the game. She hadn't known whether he had come to the same conclusions as she had, but he had certainly been very bad-tempered and by the time they had reached the first green Skye had decided that she might prefer him strained and polite after all.

The lesson had not been a great success. Skye was not a natural sportswoman, and she seemed to spend a lot of time missing the ball altogether and swinging the club helplessly round her head. Lorimer had ground his teeth and barked instructions at her until she began to giggle, which had made him even crosser. Then she had begun to get frustrated at her inability to hit that stupid little ball, and Lorimer's attempts to curb his temper and show her how to hold the club had only made *her* cross. Both had been tight-lipped when they'd left the course after nine fraught holes.

Skye settled back in her seat and watched a rabbit peer cautiously out from a hedgerow before it plucked up the courage to hop across the track and disappear into the long grass on the other side. Cautious; that was what she should be, she reflected glumly. She should think before she jumped gaily into situations that got rapidly out of control. Look where pursuing Charles had got her: stuck in a car halfway up some God-forsaken track waiting for a man who barely troubled to disguise his dislike of her.

Skye sighed. There had been a time when she had been convinced that Charles was all she wanted; now she could hardly remember what he looked like. She thought about the last time she had seen him, and then somehow she found herself thinking about how Lorimer's hands had felt against her skin. An unsettling feeling shuddered down her spine and clenched its base whenever she remembered his mouth.

Desperately trying to think of something else, anything else, Skye switched on the radio, but it was a dull programme about personal finance and kept fading off into crackles. She tried twiddling the knob, but the reception was terrible on every station, and after a while she gave up. She peered into the glove box to see if she could find any tapes instead. Reaching inside, she discovered a couple of cassettes before her hand closed over something softer and flatter. Curious, she pulled it out and turned it over. It was a silk scarf still in its presentation packet.

Skye stared down at the soft heather-coloured pattern and the way it had been folded so that the monogrammed 'M' showed through the cover. M for Moira?

What else? Lorimer was obviously waiting for the right moment to produce it as an unexpected present. It was very lovely, and would suit Moira's colouring beautifully. He must have chosen it with care.

With love?

Skye thrust the packet back into the glove box and banged it shut. It was none of her business if Lorimer wanted to buy Moira presents.

Suddenly restless, she got out of the car and stood hugging her big Peruvian knit cardigan about her against the cold. The wind blew her hair about her face and she held it back with one hand as she leant against the rickety wooden gate. Before her a rough field led down to the river, and on the far side she could just make out the granite chimneys of the Buchanans' house, half hidden in the trees. This must be part of the land Lorimer was so anxious to acquire.

It didn't look very special to Skye but on an impulse she climbed over the gate to have a closer look. It was too cold to stand still and she was too bored to get back in the car with its reminder of Moira in the glove box. It wasn't as if there was any stock to disturb, and if Lorimer was ensconced in some warm farmhouse with Duncan McPherson he could hardly object if she took a brisk walk round the field.

The turf was wet and springy beneath her feet and she soon began to regret not having boots to change into, but she plunged her hands into the pockets of her cardigan and soldiered on, enjoying the sharp wind against her face. It looked as if it had been raining recently up here, for the river was churning angrily against its banks, swirling dead branches and the odd tattered piece of plastic along with it.

Skye went closer, impressed by its energy, and curious about the lump that had come to rest against the near bank, wedged between a gnarled tree root and a trapped branch. It was a sheep, she saw, and grimaced, assuming that it had been drowned. Poor old thing, it must have fallen into the river and been swept away.

She was about to turn away when the sheep gave a feeble struggle. Caught by the branch, it couldn't quite reach the bank, and its wool was so waterlogged that it could hardly keep its head above the rushing water. Skye hesitated, biting her lip. She should really go and find the farmer, but as that was presumably Duncan McPherson Lorimer wouldn't thank her if she came bursting into the middle of his delicate negotiations. Besides, it might take ages to find them, and the wretched sheep looked on its last legs as it was. She couldn't just walk away and leave it.

Making up her mind, Skye slithered down the bank. She could see the occasional tell-tale imprint of a hoof but for the most part the bank had been trampled into a muddy mire and her shoes were already ruined.

She edged closer to the water and leant out to try and get a grip on the sheep's wool, but it was just too far away. There was nothing for it; she was going to have to get her feet wet.

The water was freezing as she stepped gingerly into the river. Gritting her teeth, Skye took another step towards the sheep and promptly sank up to her waist as the mud slipped away beneath her.

'Aagh! Aagh!' For a minute, she could do nothing but shake her hands and gasp at the shock of the intense cold rushing through her clothes. Why hadn't she at least taken her cardigan off? 'Another case of not looking before you leap,' she muttered grimly through chattering teeth. Oh, well, she was in now. She had better get on with it.

Shivering violently, she waded over to the sheep and tried to pull it free of the branch, but her presence only served to panic it into a sudden struggle that entangled it even further and managed to submerge Skye completely in the process.

She surfaced, choking and spluttering and swearing loudly. 'I'm trying to help you, you stupid animal!' It took some time, and several more dunkings, but at last she managed by a combination of pushing and dragging to get both sheep and branch to the bank where they lay equally motionless. Skye clambered out on to the mud after them, wheezing with effort.

'Come on, you can't die now,' she gasped, staggering to her feet and bending down to haul the sheep further up the bank. Somewhere in the distance there was a shout, but Skye was too busy with the sodden, uncooperative sheep to hear. Swearing fluently, she wrapped both arms round it bodily, and as if suddenly realising that there was solid earth beneath it once more the sheep erupted without warning into life. One second it was a lump, barely alive, and the next it had shot out from between her hands and was up the bank and shambling across the field without so much as a thank-you.

Thrown off balance by its sudden bolt, Skye staggered on the slippery mud, windmilling her arms like some pantomime act in a frantic attempt to stay upright, but her shoes were even wetter than the mud. They slid from beneath her and sent her crashing face down into the mud.

For a long moment, Skye simply lay there, wondering whether, if she squeezed her eyes tightly enough closed, this might all turn out to be some horrible dream, but the cold, slimy mud pressing against her nose was all too real and with an exclamation of disgust she struggled to her feet, spitting out mud and flicking it from her fingers. She was plastered in it!

'I hope you're grateful, sheep,' she muttered and lifted her head to see what had happened to it, only to find herself staring into two faces which wore identical expressions of incredulous exasperation. Lorimer was standing next to a tough, wiry-looking old man with a lined, weather-beaten face and fierce white eyebrows, and they were both staring at her as if they didn't want to believe what they were seeing.

There was a frozen pause. 'Hello,' said Skye brightly. There didn't seem to be anything else to say. She offered them both her best smile, which was returned by neither. 'What the hell do you think you're doing?' Lorimer demanded through his teeth.

'Well, there was this sheep, you see...' Skye looked around for it as if to prove her story. It was standing in the middle of the field watching her with a decidedly suspicious expression. So much for gratitude.

The farmer looked from Skye to the sheep incredulously. 'You mean to say you jumped into the burn for that old bag of bones?'

'She was drowning,' Skye tried to explain. She knew that farmers were notoriously unsentimental, but this was ridiculous. 'I couldn't just leave her there.' She glanced at the sheep once more. It was hard to believe that only a few minutes ago it had hardly been moving. 'Do you think she'll be right?'

'Oh, aye.' Duncan McPherson grunted and cast an unsympathetic glance at his sheep. 'They're tough.' A touch of malicious amusement gleamed in his eyes as he turned his attention back to Skye. 'Tougher than you, I'll be bound.'

'You're shivering,' said Lorimer abruptly. He stepped to the top of the bank and reached down his hand. 'Come on out of there,' he ordered with about as much sympathy as Duncan had shown his sheep. 'God, what a mess!' he said as Skye let herself be pulled inelegantly up the bank to stand beside him, sodden and filthy, her hair hanging in rat's-tails about her face. His hand was warm and strong and infinitely reassuring and she wanted to cling to it, but Lorimer obviously couldn't wait to let her go. Disconsolately, Skye wiped her hands against her trousers, but it only seemed to make things worse.

'I'm sorry about this, Duncan,' said Lorimer, making a worthy if not altogether successful attempt to disguise his fury. 'This is my... this is Skye Henderson.'

Skye smiled weakly, and Duncan McPherson gave a dour nod in return. 'You'd better come up to the house and get dry,' he said.

'I—I don't want to be any trouble,' she stammered between chattering teeth.

'You should have thought of that before you got out of the car,' said Lorimer with something of a snap, but he took off his tweed jacket and wrapped it round her shoulders. 'Come on, let's get moving. I don't want you on my hands with pneumonia.'

The farmhouse stood square and solid at the end of the track. Duncan stumped into the kitchen and set the kettle on an old range, before disappearing upstairs and producing an old flannelette nightdress. It had long sleeves and a high frilled neck and smelt of mothballs. 'This was my wife's,' he said gruffly, thrusting it into Skye's hands. 'Better put it on when you've washed.'

Skye squelched into the bathroom and peeled off her sodden clothes. The plumbing might look antiquated, but the water was gloriously hot and she felt much better by the time she had washed off the mud and towelled herself dry. Rubbing the worst of the wet from her hair, she pulled on the nightdress. Her slenderness was almost lost in its voluminous folds, but it was clean and warm and, best of all, dry.

When she made her way back to the kitchen, Lorimer was sitting at the wooden table with a mug of tea in his hands, talking to Duncan whose back was to the door. It wasn't often that Skye had the opportunity to watch Lorimer's face unobserved, and she hesitated, only to take a sharp breath as he smiled suddenly at something Duncan said.

As if sensing the force of her reaction, Lorimer looked over Duncan's shoulder to where Skye stood framed in the doorway, and his smile faded. Her face was scrubbed and glowing, her curls still damp and flattened to her head like a little girl's, and she was quite unconscious of the fact that the light in the hall behind her shone right through the white material of the nightdress and silhouetted her slender curves.

After a moment, Duncan noticed the change in Lorimer's expression and he swung round in his chair. 'Come away in,' he said, seeing Skye. 'I'll get you some tea.'

'Thank you,' she said nervously. The intensity in Lorimer's eyes was making her feel stupidly shy and she tried not to look at him as she took the seat that Duncan had pulled out for her. 'I'm sorry I'm giving you so much trouble.'

'It's the least I can do after you saved one of my sheep,' Duncan said grudgingly. He set a mug of tea in front of

her. 'Not that a sheep is worth much nowadays, what
with all the rules and regulations we farmers have to put
up with, but...well, I appreciate the thought.' His eyes
twinkled at her and Skye realised that he was just playing
up to his image of dour farmer, and beneath it all he
was quite pleased to have his sheep back safe and sound.
She cupped her hands round her mug and smiled back
at him.

'Did you know she was missing?'

'Aye, I'd been up to count them in their field. They're
fenced off from the burn, but there's always one that
manages to get out. I've lost a few when the water's up.
I was checking along the banks for her when I saw your
man here heading down the river from the opposite
direction.'

'I'd been up to the farmhouse,' Lorimer explained.
'But I couldn't find Duncan, so I headed back to the
car, only to find that you'd disappeared. I was not best
pleased, as you can imagine, especially not when I heard
a lot of unladylike shouting and swearing from the burn.
Duncan obviously heard it too.'

'Most unladylike,' Duncan confirmed gravely, but he
winked at Skye, who blushed and hung her head.

'At least Duncan and I have had a chance to talk while
you were in the bath,' said Lorimer, relenting. 'And
Duncan has agreed to reconsider my new proposal.'

'Oh, good.' Skye brightened. Perhaps the whole
afternoon wasn't going to turn into such a disaster after
all. 'I saw your clubs in the hall,' she said to Duncan.
'You could play every day with a golf course right on
your doorstep.'

'Farmers don't have time to play golf every day,'
Duncan grumbled. 'And I don't suppose a la-di-da

course like this one sounds will be open to the likes of me.'

'Of course it will,' said Skye stoutly, ignoring Lorimer's attempts to catch her eye. 'Why, I wouldn't be surprised if they made you an honorary member to thank you for making the course possible.'

Duncan shot a speculative look at Lorimer. 'Aye, well, there might be something in that,' he said slowly.

'I'm sure we could work something out.' Lorimer was looking resigned.

'Think how nice it would be just to stroll down the track and have a round or two whenever you felt like it,' Skye added persuasively. 'It must be lonely living up here on your own. I'm sure there would be masses of visitors who'd like to play with someone like you who *really* knows the course.'

Duncan's eyes took on a far-away look, clearly imagining how grateful visitors might like to express their appreciation of his local knowledge at the nineteenth green afterwards. 'It might not be so bad, I suppose,' he said with a sly grin at Skye. 'Do you play?'

'Yes,' she said proudly, remembering her lesson, then caught Lorimer's eye. 'Well, a bit.'

'Then perhaps we'll have a game some time.'

Skye beamed at him. 'I'd like that.'

'She'll need a bit of practice before she takes on a player like you,' said Lorimer drily. 'Sky still thinks a wood is a lot of trees and an iron is something you use when the laundry basket is full.'

Skye glanced across the table at him. A reluctant smile was tugging at the corner of his mouth and he was watching her with a mixture of amusement, resignation and exasperation...and something else that Skye couldn't identify but which made her feel hollow inside. She jerked her eyes away and cradled the mug in her hands as if she were cold.

Beneath his dour demeanour, Duncan proved to have a sardonic sense of humour and he had taken a quite unexpected liking to Skye. Prompted by her interest, he told her all about his wife and how they had struggled to keep the farm going over the years. Their only son had flatly refused to have anything to do with anything as unprofitable as a farm and, much to Duncan's disgust, had gone off to be an accountant in Dundee. Since his wife's death ten years ago, Duncan had carried grimly on by himself, unable to contemplate a different life, the sheer hard work broken only by his weekly round of golf at Kielven, half an hour's drive away.

All this he told Skye, while Lorimer pushed back his chair slightly and turned to watch them both, the tough old farmer and the vibrant girl with the sympathetic blue eyes and the curls drying in wild golden disorder around her face. When Lorimer glanced at his watch and indicated that they should be on their way, Duncan was well-embarked on a vituperative denunciation of the current agricultural policy and was disappointed to be stopped in full flight.

'Are you away back to Edinburgh?'

'No, we thought we'd stay for the presentation dinner tomorrow. You'll be there, won't you, Duncan?'

He nodded. 'I won the Kielven Cup this year,' he said proudly. 'I'm going to collect it.'

'In that case, we'll see you there,' said Lorimer. 'You'll have had a chance to think things through by then, so perhaps you could let me know then if you've decide to accept my proposal?'

But Duncan was too canny to be rushed into a sudden decision. 'I might have decided by then, but I might not,' was all he would say.

Outside, it was dark and cold and wet. 'I'd better carry you,' said Lorimer, looking down at Skye's bare feet. Duncan had insisted that she keep the nightdress for the time being and had bundled all her wet clothes into a plastic bag. When Lorimer lifted her up into his arms, Skye linked her arms awkwardly around his neck, shocked at how desperately she wanted to relax into him and bury her face against his throat. She was burningly, agonisingly aware of her nakedness beneath the night-dress, and of Lorimer's strong arms holding her easily against his chest.

Duncan stumped through the muddy farmyard beside them, carrying the bag of clothes. Once Skye was safely installed in the car, he leant through the window and shook her hand gravely in farewell. Then he nodded across at Lorimer who was inserting the key in the ignition. 'We don't want her jumping into any more burns,' he said. 'You'd better take better care of your lassie in future. She's no as silly as she looks.'

Lorimer turned to look at Skye as the engine throbbed into life and his smile glinted briefly in the lights from the dashboard. 'I'm beginning to think you might be right,' he said.

CHAPTER EIGHT

KIELVEN was a small village of huddled white-washed houses on the coast where the hills rolled down into the sea. At low tide, the water was sucked out into the Solway, the firth that divided Scotland from the hills of Cumbria, leaving behind a vast expanse of gleaming mud threaded with silver channels. You could walk for three miles out to sea on the mud flats, Lorimer had told Skye that morning, but the tide could be treacherous, rushing in at a tremendous speed and drowning unwary walkers in its dangerous currents. There were points, the locals said, where the incoming tide could overtake a man on a galloping horse.

The tide was on its way in when they got back to the hotel. Skye caused something of a stir being carried inside in Mrs McPherson's nightdress, and all conversation stopped as Lorimer set her on her feet. 'Why do you always make me feel as if I'm taking part in a bad play?' he muttered out of the corner of his mouth.

By tacit agreement, they avoided the empty dining-room and ate in the cosy bar with its crackling fire and the ranks of whisky jugs hanging from the ceiling above the bar. Skye had changed out of the nightdress, but seemed somehow just as conspicuous in jeans and a jewel-coloured jumper. Outside, the rain splattered against the windows with a rattle like a thousand tiny stones hitting the glass and whenever the door opened a great gust of wind would blow in the new arrival.

With conversation going on all around them, the atmosphere between them was easier than the night before, but, even so, Skye felt absurdly self-conscious. It was ridiculous. She had *never* been shy. It was just that desire wrenched at her whenever she caught sight of his hands around his whisky glass or his jaw with its faint prickle of stubble or the lean, decisive length of him as he leant against the bar. Skye twisted her glass desperately between her hands. She felt confused and panicky, overwhelmed by her conflicting feelings for the austere man sitting by her side.

'Are you all right?' Lorimer was watching her more closely than she knew, and she felt the treacherous colour deepen in her cheeks.

'Yes,' she said, hating how high and squeaky her voice sounded. 'At least ... it's very stuffy in here, isn't it?'

Lorimer glanced at the window. 'The rain seems to have stopped. I wouldn't mind going for a walk to clear my head either.' He drained his glass and got to his feet. 'Coming?'

He helped Skye into her jacket and she quivered at the brush of his fingers against her collar. Shrugging on his own, he held open the door and they went out into the night together.

The rain had stopped, but the wind was blowing the boats around and their halyards rattled frantically. When Skye leant over the sea wall, the water was slapping and chopping against the stones and as her eyes adjusted to the darkness she could see two wooden rowing boats straining against their buoys.

In silence, they walked past the low white-washed houses along the front and along the merse where the sea murmured just out of sight beyond the gorse bushes. The merse ended in a small shingle beach, sheltered from the worst of the wind, and Lorimer put out a hand to help Skye over the pebbles. His fingers were tight and warm over hers and for a moment she thought he was going to keep hold of her hand. The next, he had released her and she was scolding herself ferociously for letting her heart leap in such a stupid, hopeful way.

They sat together on a flat rock, listening to the waves breaking over the beach. They might have been alone in the world, Skye thought with a little shiver, surrounded by the inky blackness of the night. It had seemed dark in the village but there were no comforting lights here to chink the inky blackness. Skye could just see the froth of the waves as they crashed on to the rocks, but beyond that nothing. There was just the sound of the wind and the water, the sharp sting of spray on her face and Lorimer, still and solid beside her.

Ever since one of her brothers had shut her in a cupboard for one long, long afternoon when they were all small, Skye had hated and feared the close, claustrophobic blackness of the pitch-dark. It was one of the reasons she liked living in a city where it was never utterly dark or utterly silent. It was different here. There were no street-lamps, no passing headlights, no neighbours' televisions blaring until the small hours, only the wind and the rain and the night.

Hoping that Lorimer wouldn't notice, Skye edged a little closer to his reassuring presence. As long as he was there, she was safe, and the darkness itself was a comfort. It hid her bright, frivolous colours and made the differences between them seem unimportant. She turned her head to look at him. It was difficult to see him clearly, but she could just make out the line of his nose, the set of his jaw and the faint gleam of his eyes as he stared out into the dark, almost as if he had forgotten she was there.

Skye wondered what he was thinking about. Whatever it was, it wasn't her, she realised with a pang. 'Where's your house?' She asked the first thing that came into her head, seized by a sudden desire to remind him of her presence.

'The manse?' Lorimer seemed to rouse himself, and gestured into the darkness. 'On the other side of the bay here. I thought we'd go there tomorrow, since we've got some time to kill before the dinner.' He hesitated. 'At least...you don't have to come, if you don't want to.'

'No, I'd like to,' said Skye quickly, telling herself that she was simply curious to see the house that he had fallen in love with, and not desperate to be near him.

There was another long pause, then they both spoke at once. 'Will——?' she said at the same time as Lorimer began,

'I——'

'You first,' said Skye awkwardly.

He was silent for so long that she began to think he hadn't heard her. 'I think I owe you an apology,' he said out of the darkness at last. 'I was quite wrong to insist that you wouldn't be welcome down here because you were English,' he went on, choosing his words with care. 'The Buchanans obviously thought you were wonderful, and so did Duncan McPherson. You were the one who persuaded him to think seriously about selling his land, not me. If it hadn't been for you, I might never have had the chance to talk to him at all.' He had been looking straight ahead, but now he glanced down at Skye. 'I haven't thanked you for that. I should have done.'

'You couldn't be expected to thank me at once for disobeying all your strict instructions,' said Skye fairly and his smile gleamed briefly through the darkness.

'Knowing you as I do, I should never have expected that you *would* obey them! I just wanted to say that I was sorry,' he continued more seriously. 'I was instantly prejudiced against you just because you were English, and it made me unpleasant and unreasonable.'

Skye didn't look at him, but she was very conscious of him beside her. This was a new Lorimer and she wasn't at all sure how to deal with him or the strange new intimacy of the darkness. 'It was an understandable reaction after the experience you had with Caroline,' she said, a little hesitantly.

There was an infinitesimal pause, then Lorimer said, 'Yes...' She thought he was about to say more, but after a moment he simply repeated himself, more firmly this time, 'Yes.'

The waves smacked and sprayed over the rocks and the wind keened over the water, but Skye didn't hear them. She felt as if she and Lorimer were marooned in a bubble of silence that grew increasingly taut. She found that she was holding her breath, and let it out carefully, concentrating on the simple necessity of breathing in and out to take her mind off the sudden, urgent need to lean against him and press her lips to the faint blur of his throat, to feel his warmth and his strength and his hard, reassuring body.

In, out, in, out...just keep breathing, Skye told herself, but she was so tense that when Lorimer spoke her name hesitantly out of the darkness she froze.

'Skye?'

'Yes?' she gasped on a sharp, inward breath.

Silence. 'Nothing,' said Lorimer brusquely as if he had suddenly changed his mind. He stood up, his feet crunching on the pebbles. 'It's getting cold. Let's go back.'

Skye followed him more slowly up the beach, unsure of whether she felt relieved or agonisingly disappointed. There had been such a strange note in his voice as he said her name, and the base of her spine had clenched in a mixture of hope and panic and a wild, thrilling anticipation.

They were careful not to touch as they walked back to the inn without speaking. 'I think I'll walk on a bit,' said Lorimer gruffly as they reached the door. 'You go in.' Without waiting for her reply, he turned and strode off, leaving Skye alone in the darkness that felt cold and threatening without him.

Inside, the pub was warm and bright, and she could hear voices raised cheerfully in the bar as she climbed the stairs. At this time of year, there were few visitors, and she and Lorimer had the floor to themselves. It was colder up there, too, and Skye shivered as she washed quickly in the old-fashioned bathroom and hurried back to her room along the draughty corridor.

It was years since she had slept between sheets. The unfamiliar blankets weighed heavily on her legs, and she shifted restlessly, wondering what Lorimer had been going to say before he changed his mind so abruptly. The lights from the bar below threw a dim yellow light up through the darkness and the occasional burst of laughter made her feel less alone, and she fell asleep at last, still wondering.

She was standing on the Solway mud watching the sea racing towards her. She knew she should run, but her legs wouldn't move and beneath her feet the mud began to shift and suck her down. Suddenly Lorimer was there, on a wild-looking horse, and she stretched out her hand for him to help her, but he just galloped past, leaving her to the sea which bore relentlessly down on her, swirling her into a vicious whirlpool and dragging her down, down...

Skye woke, jerking upright as the scream stuck in her throat. Her heart hammered against her ribs as the terror lingered, and she struggled to breathe in short, jerky little gasps. Her screams lingered on and on in her mind, and it was only gradually that the nightmare faded enough for her realise that the noise she could hear was the wind, screeching around the corner of the building, while the rain threw itself ferociously at the window. Below, the lights had long been extinguished and the darkness in the room was thick and menacing and utterly still compared to the fury outside.

A vicious crack of lightning only made the blackness around Skye more absolute, and she began to shake as childhood terrors replaced those of the nightmare. It was silly to be so frightened of the dark, she tried to remind herself. It was just because of Harry and that horrible cupboard. She was perfectly safe. Still, she groped across to the bedside table and clicked the light switch.

Nothing happened.

Skye clicked it again, and again more frantically, but it was completely dead and her brave attempt at thinking rationally dissolved in the remembered fear of that afternoon seventeen years ago. Every ghastly detail was still clear in her mind: the click of the lock, the boys' giggles and whispers as they ran away, the choking, suffocating darkness and the terror that had built up inside her so that once she had started screaming it had been impossible to stop.

She *had* to get some light. It took all Skye's courage to throw back the blankets, swing her legs off the bed and step into the darkness, her arms stretched stiffly ahead of her. She walked straight into something—a chair?—which scraped across the floor, but somehow she made it to the door and fumbled for the light switch, whimpering when she found that didn't work either.

Skye had the chilling conviction that she had woken to find that the nightmare was real after all, and her precarious control slipped as she panicked and grappled for the door, terrified of remaining alone in this malevolent blackness. If she could just find Lorimer, she would be safe. The mere thought of him was enough to steady her and she edged along the wall of the corridor. There had been a light switch out here somewhere, but where? *Where*?

The sound of the storm was muted in the windowless corridor, and her own rasping breathing sounded eerie and unnaturally loud as she felt along the wall for the switch. Disorientated, she tried to remember where Lorimer's room was, and found that she was muttering, 'Please let me find him, please, please, please,' under her breath like an incantation.

Her hand closed over a handle, and she turned it with shaking fingers just as a sharp click behind her made her whirl round with a stifled scream.

'Skye?' Lorimer's voice spoke out of the darkness and Skye burst into overwrought tears.

'I'm here, I'm here,' she sobbed, stumbling towards the sound of his voice. He must have taken a step towards her, for she came smack up against the infinite reassurance of his hard body and clutched frantically at him, giving a great sigh of relief as Lorimer's arms closed tightly about her.

'Skye? What is it?' he asked, his voice rough with anxiety at her obvious distress, but Skye couldn't speak. She could only shudder and burrow her face into the hollow between his throat and his shoulder.

He had pulled on a pair of trousers, but his chest was bare and Skye clung to his warm, sleek strength as if it was her only refuge. She was wearing a frivolous satin nightdress, and she could feel his hands smoothing rhythmically over the flimsy material, burning through to her skin with their hard reassurance as he murmured soothingly against her soft hair.

'What is it?' Lorimer asked again when her terrified sobs had subsided into hiccuping gasps. He made as if to draw back slightly so that he could look down into her face but Skye's arms tightened instinctively around his back in panic.

'The dark,' she muttered into his shoulder, just becoming aware of his warm, bare skin but unable to face the prospect of letting go.

'The storm must have brought down an electricity pole.' She could hear his voice rumbling in his chest as he spoke. 'None of the lights is working. What were you doing out here if you're afraid of the dark?'

Skye's eyelashes flickered against his skin. 'Looking for you,' she whispered. 'But I couldn't remember where your room was.'

'It's just as well I heard you, in that case,' he said, a dry edge to his voice. 'You were heading in quite the wrong direction. I heard something crash over in your room, and then whimpering out here, so I thought I'd better come and see what was going on. It was only when I tried my switch that I realised the lights were off.' He had been rubbing his hand gently up and down her spine as if soothing a scared animal, but he paused now and Skye heard the frown in his voice. 'You're shivering! Come on, let's get you back to bed.'

He kept one arm about her as he guided her back to her room and felt through the darkness for her bed. 'Here we are,' he said, locating it at last and throwing back the blankets. 'In you get.'

Skye sat down, then clutched at him, panicking at the thought of being left alone again. 'You won't go?' she pleaded, and then, as he hesitated, '*Please*, Lorimer.' She hated the tearful waver to her voice, but it was too late for pride now. 'I know it's stupid, but...please don't go.'

'All right, I'll stay,' said Lorimer with a sigh, pushing her down on to the pillow. 'But only if you get into bed right now.' He sounded brusque, but his hands were tender as he tucked her in and then lay down beside her, drawing the eiderdown up to cover them both. Shifting himself into a more comfortable position, he lifted his arm wordlessly to let Skye snuggle up against him. When she was settled, he let his arm enclose her, smoothing his thumb almost absently over her silken skin while she listened to the slow, steady, infinitely reassuring beat of his heart.

'Thank you,' she said very quietly after a while, when her own heartbeat had calmed.

'My pleasure,' said Lorimer in a wry voice, and then, in a quite different tone, 'Do you want to talk about it?'

Skye swallowed. She felt warm and comfortable and safe in his arms, as if she had come home after a long journey. 'It's silly,' she mumbled into his chest.

'It can't be that silly,' said Lorimer. 'You were rigid with terror out there in the corridor, and you're not the kind of girl who bursts into tears over nothing.'

Slowly, haltingly, Skye told him about being shut in the cupboard. She told him of her fear and her panic and the shame she felt at her irrational phobia. 'It sounds so babyish, being afraid of the dark,' she said in a small voice. 'And I don't mind usually, when there's enough light from street-lamps or the moon. It's just the pitch-dark that terrifies me, like the cupboard, or waking up tonight.'

'Or the stairs up to your flat?' Lorimer said above her head, and his hand tightened suddenly on her shoulder in self-recrimination. 'You told me you were afraid of the dark, and I didn't believe you then.'

Skye lay very still, remembering. She remembered how he had jeered, how he had taken her in his arms and kissed her and left her shaken by the passion he had unleashed within her. Was Lorimer remembering too? She was agonisingly aware of him, his broad bare chest beneath her cheek, his hand smoothing over her arm, the beat of his heart and the warmth of his skin, and the slippery satin that was all there was between them. She wished Lorimer hadn't mentioned the incident in her darkened hallway. She had just been beginning to relax, and now her nerves were strumming again, although this time it was not with fear.

'You weren't to know that I was really frightened,' she said in a low voice. 'I wouldn't have told you tonight if you hadn't seen me crying like a baby. I feel so stupid...' She trailed off and he lifted his hand to stroke the curls tangling softly beneath his chin.

'There's no need to feel embarrassed about it. We all have secret fears.'

'I bet you don't,' said Skye in a rather muffled voice. It was still absolutely dark, but Lorimer's arms about her kept every fear at bay. He was so decisive, so invulnerable, that it was impossible to imagine that he could be afraid of anything.

'Not now, perhaps, but it doesn't mean I can't remember what it was like.' His fingers were entwined in her hair and she could feel his chest rising and falling steadily beneath her arm. His thoughts seemed to be far away. 'Do you know why I was so prejudiced against you when I first met you, Skye?' he asked after a long moment.

'Because of Caroline ruining all your plans?'

'There was that, but my distrust of the English goes back a long way before Caroline. I told you I grew up not far from Glendorie; I didn't tell you that my mother left my father for an Englishman when I was eight.' He paused. Skye said nothing, but her arm tightened slightly around him, thinking of an unhappy and bewildered little boy.

'My father was very bitter,' Lorimer went on at last. 'Richard had been a friend of his, and that betrayal of trust hurt him nearly as much as my mother's. I stayed with my father in Scotland and I suppose I absorbed a lot of his bitterness. It taught me to be very cynical about marriage. Theirs had seemed so happy on the surface, but obviously it had been no more than a charade. I think my father realised that too. After my mother left, he just didn't care about anything any more, and I was left to run pretty wild. He died a couple of years later, by which time I was almost uncontrollable, and my mother was horrified when she came to take me away to live with her and Richard in Surrey. I didn't want to go, and I don't think they wanted to have me much either.

I was homesick and determined to hate everything about England, and in the end they sent me away to school— to civilise me, they said.' Lorimer's voice was bitter. 'That was even worse. I was tormented about my accent and bullied mercilessly for being different. I tried to run away three times, but I never got very far. I cried myself to sleep every night.'

Skye was swept by a wave of tenderness for the unhappy little boy Lorimer had been. She tilted her head slightly and laid her palm against his cheek. 'Poor little boy,' she said gently.

'I survived.' Lorimer's fingers resumed caressing her soft hair. 'I've never told anyone that before,' he said thoughtfully. 'In fact, I probably didn't realise quite how much my attitudes towards the English had been affected by what happened. Not talking about it to anyone just made things worse. I'd have been very wary of marriage in any case, but perhaps I should have realised sooner that it's stupid to generalise about nationalities. My mother could have run off with another Scot, and the misery would have been the same. Prejudices are just excuses for our own unhappiness, and it certainly wasn't fair of me to take them out on you.' Lorimer hesitated. 'That's really what I wanted to say at the beach.'

'You didn't need to apologise,' said Skye. 'Nobody could blame you for hating the English after an experience like that. It's funny, I never thought of myself as being particularly English before, but I suppose I am.'

'You are.' There was a hint of amusement in Lorimer's voice. 'You couldn't be anything else.'

'I'll try and be less English from now on,' she offered.

'I don't think you should change,' he said firmly. 'Not when I've just got used to you the way you are.'

'Wouldn't you like a man to love you for being the way you are?'

Why should she remember Vanessa's words now? Lorimer had only said he was used to her. It was a long way from loving her, but still Skye felt a glow simmer and burn along her veins until it beat insistently under her skin. Her hands itched with the need to drift over his tautly muscled body. She wanted to turn in his arms and let her lips drift up his throat to his mouth. She wanted him to pull her roughly beneath him and explore her eager body with his mouth and his hands. She wanted him to kiss her and tell her that he was more than used to her, that he wanted her and needed her just as she needed him.

Lorimer didn't seem to notice the way her slender body thrummed in his arms. He yawned. Making love to her was evidently the last thing on his mind, Skye realised in humiliation.

'It's late,' he said. 'Do you think you'll be all right on your own now? Or do you want me to stay?' he added in a dry voice as she clutched at him in instinctive panic at the suggestion that he might leave.

Skye knew that she ought to let him go back to his own room, but the darkness seemed to leer at her from outside the circle of Lorimer's arms. The storm shrieked and rattled the window as if auditioning for the sound effects on a horror film. It would be very dark and very cold and very lonely in here without him.

'Would you mind staying?' she asked in a small voice, lifting her head to peer doubtfully through the darkness into his face.

She caught the brief gleam of a smile as Lorimer brought her head back down to his shoulder. 'No, I don't mind,' he said.

* * *

Skye woke slowly, aware of an unfamiliar sense of security and blissful comfort but too content to wonder as she stirred and stretched sleepily.

'At last! I thought you were going to sleep all day.'

Lorimer's dry voice brought Skye fully awake and her eyes flicked open. She was lying pressed against his side, her head on his chest and her arm flung possessively across him, but even as her gaze focused Lorimer was lifting his arm from around her and sitting up.

The events of last night flooded back and Skye's cheeks were tinged pink with embarrassment as she struggled to disentangle herself from him. 'Y-you should have woken me,' she stammered awkwardly.

'I didn't like to. You were dead to the world, and I thought you'd be exhausted after last night.' Lorimer stretched and flexed his shoulders as he drew the curtains. The storm had miraculously blown itself out and the sky was blue and bright, dispelling the last gloom of the long night. 'Besides,' he said, turning back to her with a half-smile, 'you look very peaceful when you're sleeping.'

Skye was very conscious of his bare chest, of her frivolously revealing nightdress and the unbearable intimacy of the rumpled sheets, and she dropped her eyes, feeling the colour deepen in her cheeks.

'I'm sorry about last night,' she said with difficulty.

Lorimer crossed back to the bed and sat down on the edge, studying her averted face. 'There's no need to apologise.'

'Well . . . thank you for being so understanding.' Skye swallowed. 'It must have been very uncomfortable for you to have me clinging to you like a limpet all night.'

Lorimer's grin was rather twisted. 'Uncomfortable is one word for it,' he agreed with a cryptic look. 'I can think of others.'

Skye turned her head almost unwillingly to meet his eyes and there was a pregnant silence as they looked at each other. Suddenly Lorimer got to his feet. 'I'm going to dress. You'd better do the same if you don't want to miss breakfast. I'll see you in the dining-room.'

It wasn't the most romantic exit line, but his prosaic words helped dissolve some of Skye's awkwardness, and by the time she had showered and dressed she felt quite herself again. She found Lorimer, as promised, in the dining-room, drinking coffee and reading *The Scotsman*, but he looked up and smiled as she came in.

Skye felt a reckless happiness balloon and blossom inside her. She had been afraid that the humiliating fear of the night, and the embarrassment of waking up in his arms, would make things awkward between them, but if anything it had dissolved the ever-present strain of their relationship and left them both oddly light-hearted.

True, Lorimer called Skye to order for talking too much and distracting him while he was trying to read his paper, but his heart wasn't really in it and he was unable to hide his grin as he folded it up with a long-suffering air and laid it aside.

They had a day to fill before the presentation dinner that evening, and Lorimer proposed that they should ask Mrs Brodie for some sandwiches and a Thermos of coffee so that they could have lunch at the manse. Skye agreed happily, but she would have been happy to do anything he suggested that morning.

Outside the air was diamond-bright and the sea glittered silver in the winter sunshine. An irresistible exhilaration seeped along Skye's veins as she waited for

Lorimer to unlock the car, stamping her feet against the cold and blowing on her fingers. She wore bright leggings, a bulky, vividly patterned jumper and a pink beret set jauntily on her wild curls. Colourful wooden tropical fish swing inappropriately from her ears.

The road dipped and rolled inland before they could turn off towards the coast once more. They drove between emerald-green fields scattered with gorse bushes and grey granite outcrops, the low heather-covered hills behind them and the silver firth ahead. Skye was chattering excitedly, invigorated by the sharp, clean air and Lorimer's amused presence beside her, but when he turned up a rough track and drew up outside the manse she could only stare in silence.

It seemed to grow out of the ground, a safe, solid white-washed house with a black door and black windows and a row of dormer windows like raised eyebrows in the roof. Set snugly back into the hill on a headland, it looked across to England on one side and across the estuary on the other to the hills rolling down into the sea until they faded into the blue distance. The garden was little more than a rough field, and at the bottom a path led down a steep cliff-path to a tiny cove with round pink and grey pebbles and a narrow strip of golden beach between the rocks.

'Well?' Lorimer switched off the engine and turned to look at Skye. There was the merest trace of anxiety in his voice but Skye was still staring at the manse and didn't notice. 'It's not like you to have nothing to say! What do you think?'

Skye took a deep breath. 'It's beautiful,' she said and then, without thinking, 'It's almost as if it's been waiting for me.' Too late, she realised how Lorimer might misinterpret her words. This wasn't her house; it never would be. 'I mean...'

'I know what you mean,' said Lorimer, amused. 'I felt that way myself.'

'It just seems a very welcoming house,' Skye tried to explain, hoping that he didn't think she was assuming some kind of claim over the house before she had even been inside. 'It's the sort of house where you know you could walk in and there would be a warm fire and tea and scones.'

Lorimer grinned as he got out of the car. 'You won't find any tea and scones today, I'm afraid. I've had the builders in all summer trying to make the place habitable, but there's still a long way to go before cosy teas around the fire!'

Skye saw what he meant as he showed her around the house. It was bigger than it appeared from the outside, with large, light rooms downstairs and a warren of little passageways, and a smell of plaster and new pipes pervaded every room. Most of the floors seemed to have been replaced and their footsteps echoed on the bare boards as they wandered from room to room.

They ate their sandwiches sitting on the doorstep in the weak November sun, sharing the coffee from the top of the Thermos in companionable silence. Afterwards, Lorimer took her for a walk along the coastal path, scrambling over lichened rocks and stepping gingerly between gorse bushes. Fat seagulls preened themselves on the rocks below or wheeled overhead screeching importantly to each other. One stubborn, solitary tree clung to the top of a cliff, so beaten and battered by the wind that it grew leaning backwards at an impossible angle, its thorny branches streamlined against the gales.

Last night's rain had washed the air so clear that they could see for miles, and across the Solway the hills of Cumbria stood out so clearly that Skye felt as if she could reach out and touch them. Her eyes reflected the crisp blue sky, and the cold gave her face a glow of colour as she slithered down a narrow path behind Lorimer to a flat, sandy beach. The tide was on its way out, leaving shallow puddles of gleaming water on the mud flats, and they picked their way between the rock pools and the seaweed to jump down on the firm sand.

Wandering slowly, aimlessly, along the shoreline, Skye stooped to pick up delicate pink butterfly shells while Lorimer tossed a round, flat pebble from hand to hand, sending it skimming over the water when they reached a channel. He was wearing jeans and a thick dark jumper that seemed to intensify the colour of his eyes, and he looked younger and happier than Skye had ever seen him.

Suddenly seized by the exhilaration of the cold and the light and the warmth in Lorimer's face, she turned a couple of cartwheels on the sand. Breathless, laughing, she came upright to find Lorimer watching her with a smile. The wind was ruffling his dark hair and his eyes looked very deep and very blue.

Skye's stomach seemed to disappear as she looked at him, and the truth, so obvious that it was hard to believe it had taken her so long to admit it to herself, hit her with the force of a blow.

She was in love with him.

CHAPTER NINE

WHAT a fool she had been! Skye turned away, her exhilaration draining rapidly into the realisation that she was on new and uncertain ground. She had claimed to be in love many times, but she had never felt like this before. This was no passing attraction; it was a deep, aching need, an instinctive knowledge that could not be denied. She wanted Lorimer, for always, forever.

What was it Vanessa had said about always falling for the wrong kind of man? 'What you need is to fall *really* in love,' she had said. Well, now she had found the right kind of man, the only man for her, and she had fallen in love, just as Vanessa had said she should. The trouble was that she was quite the wrong kind of girl for Lorimer.

Oh, he had been kinder and nicer this weekend than she would ever have thought possible, but he wasn't in love with her and he never would be. He had made it very clear that he wasn't interested in marriage, and it would take more than a silly, frivolous girl like her to change his mind. If Lorimer ever chose a wife, it would be a sensible, intelligent, reliable girl who wouldn't annoy him or embarrass him. A girl like Moira Lindsay. Bleakly, Skye remembered the scarf Lorimer kept hidden in the glove box of his car, and a hand seemed to close around her heart.

She was very quiet as they climbed back up the cliff-path and turned back to the manse in unspoken agreement. Lorimer shot her one or two curious looks, but her change of mood had created a new strain between them, and he said nothing, only dug his hands deeper into his pockets and kept his eyes on the distant hills.

Once back at the house, he excused himself to check on what the builders had been doing, and Skye was left to wander around the house, torturing herself with might-have-beens. She could imagine how it would be with a painful clarity: the house warm and decorated, a little shabby perhaps, not too tidy. Isobel Buchanan had been right when she'd called it a family house. It needed children laughing and shouting and arguing and pounding up and down the corridors.

Skye closed her eyes, shocked at how easily she could visualise Lorimer's son: a little boy with dark hair and Lorimer's eyes, the eyes that made her heart twist with love, but without the guarded, unhappy expression that he must have worn as a child.

She opened her eyes abruptly, wincing at the pain the thought of that little boy brought her. She might be able to imagine him with devastating clarity, but if he ever existed he wouldn't be her son. He would live in this lovely house and belong to quite a different woman. It was just what Lorimer needed, a loving wife and a child of his own to teach him that marriage didn't have to mean bitterness and betrayal. If only she could be the one to show him what happiness could be! Skye's eyes darkened. What was the point in taunting herself with wishing? There was no future for her with Lorimer, none at all.

Wherever she went, the images taunted her. She could see herself in the kitchen with its bright light and its windows looking out to the hills, in the dining-room, in the hall. She stood in the sitting-room for a long time, staring at the fireplace, picturing it ablaze, the curtains closed against the wind and the rain, a dog asleep on the hearthrug, eyebrows twitching as it dreamt, and Lorimer relaxed in a deep armchair, watching the flames. And then, in her imagination, he looked up and smiled and it was Skye herself who came into the room to sit at his feet and rest her head against his knee and feel his fingers tangle lovingly in her hair.

She could hear Lorimer's footsteps above her. Skye shook herself free of the dream and went upstairs. She felt empty and desolate, unable to imagine how life would be without him. She meant to find Lorimer and force herself to talk normally about everyday things, to pretend that nothing had changed, but somehow her feet faltered as they passed the main bedroom and her hand reached out of its own volition to turn the handle.

It was a big room looking out across the estuary to the hills beyond, empty except for a few bits of copper pipe and a pile of planks stacked against the wall. Skye didn't see them. She was imagining how the room would look with a wide bed, what it would be like to lie there with Lorimer, knowing that she only had to reach out to touch him, to feel his hands running possessively over her curves and his smile against her skin.

The image was so vivid that Skye squeezed her eyes shut involuntarily against the pain of knowing that it would never be. She had never imagined that love could hurt this much. To her horror, she realised that her cheeks were wet and she took a shuddering breath. She could hear Lorimer's footsteps ringing along the corridor outside, pausing at the open door, advancing in the room. Hastily, she turned towards the window, brushing the tears from her cheeks with the back of her hand.

'What's the matter?' Lorimer asked sharply.

'Nothing . . . nothing.'

He walked across to her and took her by the shoulders. 'What do you mean, *nothing*? You've been crying!'

'I haven't!' Sky scrubbed furiously at her face. 'I was just thinking.'

'What about?'

How could she tell him the truth? Skye wondered what he would say if she told him that she was in love with him. She didn't think she could bear to see the look of horror that would dawn in his eyes, the instinctive recoil or, worse, a kind of explanation of how it could never be. She knew that already.

'I was just . . . thinking about how things never work out as you expect,' she said at last, and to her surprise Lorimer's expression hardened as his hands fell from her shoulders.

'I suppose that means you've been crying over Charles Ferrars? I keep forgetting that he's the reason you're here, but you don't, do you?' Lorimer said harshly. 'What's the matter? Hasn't he succumbed to your wiles yet? You'll have to work a bit harder!'

Skye stared at him miserably, taken aback by the suppressed anger in his voice. She was tempted to tell him that she hadn't given Charles a thought for weeks, but what was the point? Let him think that she was still obsessed with Charles; at least it would save the embarrassment of him realising that *he* was the man haunting her dreams.

'Thanks for the advice,' she said flatly.

They glared at each other, helpless before the antagonism which had flared so suddenly between them again. A muscle twitched angrily in Lorimer's jaw and he made as if to step towards her, before changing his mind and turning away instead.

'We'd better go,' he said in the same flat tone she had used.

Skye followed him downstairs and out to the car in silence. The winter sun hung huge and glowing above the hills to the west, gleaming on the shallow puddles on the mud and turning the deeper channels to molten gold. The wind had dropped and there was an unearthly stillness to the air, as if the dusk were trembling in anticipation of the sun's final disappearance behind the hills. The temperature had dropped dramatically with the sun, and Skye could see her breath cloud in the cold air as she stood with her hands on the car door. The chill set her teeth on edge and intensified the haunting smell of woodsmoke and gorse.

She didn't want to get in the car and drive away from this house with its welcoming rooms and tempting dreams, but Lorimer was leaning over to open the door impatiently and with a last look around she got in. The time for dreams was over.

Skye never forgot the night of the presentation dinner. It was one of the longest and most miserable evenings of her life, but no one would have guessed from her bright smile and determinedly cheerful conversation. She was conscious of being hopelessly overdressed in a flared, strapless dress of a particularly vibrant shade of jade, but it was just too bad, she told herself desolately. Lorimer was always going to think of her as impossibly frivolous and out of place anyway.

Lorimer himself was in a strange mood all evening, as if he was keeping some strong emotion in check by sheer will-power. Skye took one look at his clenched jaw and shuttered eyes and put on her most brilliant smile. She scintillated over dinner, although the grey Galloway beef and overcooked vegetables tasted like ashes in her mouth, knowing that for all the attention Lorimer paid her she might as well not have been there. It was left to the Buchanans to introduce her around.

The various cups and prizes won by members of the golf club over the year were presented after dinner with mercifully short speeches. Skye applauded dutifully, and with real enthusiasm when Duncan McPherson stumped up to receive a huge cup, but she was relieved when it was over and the long tables were pushed back to make room for the reels.

The accordion and the fiddle struck up the first tune, but it was Duncan, not Lorimer, who swept her off to dance. Skye had never taken part in a reel before, but she had always loved dancing, and picked up the steps quickly. Out of the corner of her eye, she saw Lorimer lead Isobel Buchanan on to the floor. He hadn't looked at her once.

Skye's smile was dazzling as she concentrated on showing Lorimer that she was having the time of her life and couldn't care in the least that he hadn't asked her to dance. She whirled and whooped and was swung round by a succession of horny-handed farmers until her face ached with the effort of smiling.

The more Lorimer ignored her, the more vivacious Skye became. She danced every dance, and it was not until they were halfway through the Dashing White Sergeant that she suddenly found herself face to face with him. If he could, she was sure he would have stepped aside with a shudder, but the momentum of the dance was irresistible, and as the couples on either side of them were swinging Lorimer had no alternative but to take her hands and turn her as well.

'For God's sake, stop bouncing up and down and whooping like a siren,' he hissed. 'There's no need to draw everybody's attention to the fact that you've no idea what you're doing.'

Skye, burningly conscious of the touch of his hands, merely stuck out her tongue and directed a brilliant smile at the next man as Lorimer let her go and moved on. After that, she made an extra effort to let him know just how much she was enjoying herself without him, but infuriatingly Lorimer gave no sign that he even noticed. Instead, he devoted himself to his partners, including a very pretty girl who looked rather like Moira and who Skye loathed on sight. Why couldn't he ask *her* to dance?

Having danced indefatigably, Skye was flushed and breathless by the time the band changed to a slower tune to end the evening.

'You do look as if you've been having a good time,' said Isobel Buchanan approvingly. 'It's so nice to see someone who's not afraid to enjoy herself. I think you've won a few hearts tonight!'

She hadn't won the only one that mattered, Skye thought miserably. 'Everyone's been so nice,' she said, mustering another smile and pointedly not looking at Lorimer, who was talking to Angus Buchanan.

It was a relief to stand still and catch her breath, but as the band responded to appeals and struck up another slow tune Angus turned to his wife. 'My dance, I think, my dear,' he said gallantly.

'How lovely!' said Isobel with a smile and then glanced from Lorimer to Skye. 'Here's your chance to ask Skye at last, Lorimer. I've seen the way you've been watching her all evening when you haven't had a chance to get near her!'

Her husband whirled her off, and Lorimer and Skye were left trying to avoid looking at each other. Skye stared desperately out at the dancers. She longed for Lorimer to take her in his arms, but it was only too obvious that it was the last thing he wanted.

'Shall we?' he said stiffly after a moment.

'All right.' Skye knew that she sounded sulky, but she was humiliated by the fact that it had taken Isobel's heavy hint to practically force him into asking her to dance.

'You don't sound very enthusiastic,' he said as they edged on to the floor.

'It wasn't a very enthusiastic invitation!'

'What do you expect?' said Lorimer irritably. 'You've been making an exhibition of yourself all evening. I'm not likely to fall victim to that smile of yours like all those other poor fools you've been flirting with. I'm only too aware that you'd rather be snuggling up to Charles Ferrars!'

He hesitated before he put out his arms almost reluctantly and took one of her hands in his, setting the other in the small of her back. They held each other rigidly, trying to touch as little as possible, but the lights were dim and the dance-floor crowded, and it was inevitable that they would get pushed together in spite of themselves.

Skye kept her eyes fixed on Lorimer's throat, hypnotised by the steady pulse that beat there and the feel of his hand, hard against her spine. The urge to relax against him and rest her face against his neck was almost overwhelming as desire uncoiled insidiously deep within her, whispering that this might be the last time he ever held her in his arms. Surely it wouldn't matter if she leant just a little closer?

Slowly, very slowly, she succumbed to temptation, relaxing her body until the gap between their bodies was closed and she could lean her cheek against his throat at last with a tiny sigh of fulfilment. She kept waiting for Lorimer to thrust her away, but the pressure of his hand against her spine had increased imperceptibly, almost reluctantly, to bring her closer while his hold on her hand had tightened and his head lowered so that he could lay his cheek against her soft, shining hair.

Skye could feel herself pounding with desire. Part of her wanted this moment to go on forever, but the rest of her longed to be able to turn her head and feel his lips against hers. She wanted him to take her upstairs and make love to her. She wanted to taste his skin and feel the glorious hardness of his body beneath her fingers.

Neither wish was to be granted. All too soon, the tune drew to an end and the company broke into a rousing chorus of 'Auld Lang Syne'. Skye found herself standing by herself, blinking stupidly at the smiling faces around her while her hands were seized and pumped enthusiastically up and down by perfect strangers.

She couldn't believe that Lorimer could sound so normal as they said goodbye to the Buchanans outside. She supposed she must have smiled and said goodbye automatically, but she felt disjointed and disorientated, her senses still clamouring for Lorimer's touch. It was a clear night and the cold was hardening into frost. Skye was grateful for the darkness which hid her dazed expression and for the chill air on her burning skin, cooling her senses and bringing her back to reality.

She stood next to Lorimer without speaking, without touching, as they watched the Buchanans drive away. 'Well, I . . . I think I'll go to bed,' she said awkwardly.

Lorimer glanced down at her with a sardonic look, but he said nothing as they went back inside and climbed the stairs. Below, they could hear the cheerful sounds of the last farewells and the band packing up, but here in the dim corridor the atmosphere was one of silent, strumming tension.

Skye's pulse hammered in her throat and she clutched the key to her room like a talisman against the wild heat of desire, craving Lorimer's touch but terrified of what she might reveal if he did.

'That was quite a display down there,' said Lorimer tightly, shattering the fraught silence as they stopped outside her door.

'Wh-what do you mean?'

'I've got to hand it to you, Skye,' he said, his expression hard and contemptuous. 'You certainly know how to play the warm, desirable woman—or is it that you get lots of practice?'

'I don't know what you're talking about.'

'Don't you? Clinging to me in that seductive night-dress, begging me to stay all night, and, just now, melting in my arms, so warm and so soft... and so determined to get another man! It's just as well I know all about your obsession with Charles Ferrars or I might be starting to get the wrong ideas about you, Skye. What a pity for you that Charles wasn't here last night to witness your display of helplessness! You must have been cursing the wasted opportunity when you had to spend the night in my arms instead of his!'

'Oh, I don't know,' said Skye coldly. Lorimer's sneers had done more than anything else to drive all thought of desire from her mind and leave her icily angry and determined to hurt him as much as he was hurting her.

'Anyone would have done. You just happened to be conveniently there.'

Lorimer's eyes narrowed dangerously. 'So I was convenient, was I? How handy for you to have a *convenient* man to practise you seduction technique on!' His hands shot out and jerked her towards him. 'Perhaps you'd like to practise some more?'

'No!' The key fell unheeded to the floor as Skye struggled against him but his arms were like steel bands around her.

'No?' he mocked. 'That wasn't the message I was getting on the dance-floor.'

'Let me go!'

'No, I don't think I will,' said Lorimer in a silky voice, tightening his grip. 'I feel like a little practice myself.' He took her chin in one hand and turned her stormy face up to his. 'That's only fair, isn't it?'

The next instant his mouth came down on hers in a hard punishing kiss. Skye rammed her hands against his chest, but his only response was to gather her closer and all of sudden the whole quality of the kiss changed. The bitterness and the anger had dissolved imperceptibly into a sweetness that caught them both unawares, and swept the kiss beyond their control on a surging tide of intoxicating delight.

The hard, hurtful words they had flung at each other were forgotten. It was as if their bodies had a will of their own, succumbing to a much greater force as the sweetness exploded into a rocketing excitement and their mouths explored each other in deepening desire and acknowledgement of mutual need.

Skye's arms slid around his neck and her fingers tangled in his hair, hardly noticing as they fell back against the wall, still kissing desperately. Lorimer's hands were moving urgently over her body, beneath her dress, hard and demanding against the swell of her breast, the warmth of her thigh, sliding with tantalising assurance over her silken skin. Skye clung to him hungrily, her senses reeling, abandoned utterly to the electrifying delight of Lorimer's touch and Lorimer's taste and the hard, thrilling promise of Lorimer's body.

When his mouth left hers, she moaned in protest, only to shudder as his lips travelled enticingly along her jaw. 'How does it feel to be used?' he murmured against her ear.

It took several seconds for Skye to absorb what he had said. She went absolutely cold. Jerking her arms down from around his neck, she would have recoiled, but he still held her in hands that were suddenly cruel.

'That *wasn't* fair,' she whispered.

'Now you know what it's like,' said Lorimer with a tight smile. 'It's not nice being used, is it?'

Skye fought her way free of him at last. 'I haven't used you!'

'Oh, come on, Skye. You've made no secret of how you feel about Charles. I can remember reluctantly admiring your honesty—but that was before I knew that I was destined to act as a poor substitute!'

'You, a substitute for Charles?' How could he kiss her like that one moment and jeer at her so bitterly the next? 'Don't make me laugh!' Skye lashed out, too hurt to know or care what she was saying. 'You couldn't begin to be an adequate substitute for him!'

'Really?' Lorimer was as angry as she was. 'How does Charles kiss you, Skye? Like this?' He pulled her back into his arms, tormenting her with searing kisses that left Skye trembling and helpless. 'Or like this?' His voice altered, and this time when his lips met hers they were gentle and persuasive and indescribably tender. He kissed her as if he loved her, as if she was a rare and precious thing, and Skye had no defences left to resist. She was bewitched, enchanted, leaning into him with a sigh and letting her hands creep up to hold his face as she felt herself dissolve in unimaginable sweetness.

The disappointment when he released her was so agonising that she had to bite back a cry of pain. She stared up at him, devastated, humiliated. He must know how utterly she had succumbed, fool that she was. He must realise how she had let herself believe that this time the kiss was for real. He must know now that her angry words had been no more than bluff and that she had nothing left to fight him with.

But Lorimer's expression was unreadable. 'Perhaps you're right,' he said. 'It's not quite the same as kissing someone you love, is it?'

Skye flinched. Had he been comparing her to Moira all the time? His callous words tore her heart slowly, deliberately, excruciatingly apart, and her knees trembled uncontrollably as she bent to pick up her key from the carpet. 'No,' she said shakily, wondering how long she could keep the bitter tears at bay. 'I suppose it isn't.'

They barely exchanged a word on the way back to Edinburgh the next morning. It was another beautiful day with a hard, glittering frost rimming the grass and lacing the stark outlines of the trees. Skye stared unseeingly out of her window and wondered whether loving Lorimer would ever stop hurting. Would it recede to a dull, nagging ache in time, or would she always have to put up with this vicious, clawing pain whenever she thought of him? She felt raw and wretched, lacerated by memories of that last treacherous kiss. Did Lorimer realise how much he had hurt her by kissing her with such tenderness? Did he know how bitter her disillusion had been when she realised that it had meant nothing to him at all, *nothing*?

Vanessa took one look at Skye's face when she came in the door and wisely said nothing. Skye was grateful for her understanding; she didn't think she could have talked about Lorimer even if she had wanted to. Her throat felt too tight, her mind too numb. She sat in front of the television all afternoon, gazing blankly at the flickering screen without hearing a word, but doing nothing only gave her the opportunity to think, so she agreed when Vanessa suggested going out that evening. She was going to have to get on with her life some time; she might as well start now.

Skye sat in the crowded pub with Vanessa and her friends and made a heroic effort to look cheerful. She talked and laughed and whenever her mind veered towards Lorimer or the house waiting quietly between the sea and the hills she would resolutely push the image aside. Still, it was a relief to walk home through the dark streets with Vanessa and stop smiling.

They were walking up the High Street towards the castle when Skye saw Lorimer. He was standing on the kerb, hailing a taxi, and Moira was standing next to him, laughing up at something he had said. She looked happy, glowing, in love.

Skye's heart twisted in pain and she stepped back into a dark doorway. Not that there was any fear that Lorimer would look across the road and see her. He was too preoccupied with the beautiful girl by his side, putting his hand out solicitously to see her into the taxi, smiling as he climbed in after her. The taxi switched off its light and rumbled off over the cobbles.

Her last hope, that Lorimer's bitter words and furious kisses might have been born of jealousy, died on the dark pavement there. What reason would he have to be jealous when he had a girl like Moira, so radiantly in love? There was no mistaking her happiness, nor Lorimer's smiles. He didn't look bitter or cynical with Moira. He didn't look like a man who had shunned the very thought of marriage. He looked like a man who was well on his way to deciding that marriage was exactly what he wanted after all.

'Do you want to talk about it?' asked Vanessa quietly.

'No.' Skye could hear her voice cracking. 'I—I can't. Not yet.'

From somewhere deep inside her, she dredged some vestige of pride. Lorimer didn't love her, would never love her. She would just have to accept that, and get through the last three weeks before Christmas with as much dignity as she could. That meant not letting Lorimer guess for one moment just how much he had come to mean to her.

On Monday, she and Lorimer were meticulously polite to each other. The weekend wasn't referred to once. It might never have happened at all, Skye thought, drawing her keyboard towards her and beginning on the huge pile of scribbled letters Lorimer had produced that morning. He must have spent all of yesterday afternoon writing them. She would have thought he'd have been so desperate to see Moira that he would have had no time for work.

She was typing out a letter to the solicitor about the proposed purchase of Duncan McPherson's land when the door opened and Moira Lindsay came in. She was wearing a neat skirt and a grey round-necked jumper set off to perfection by the subtle tones of a silk scarf.

Skye recognised it at once. It was the scarf Lorimer had secreted in his car. Obviously the right moment had come last night.

Moira smiled at Skye who dully noted the glow of happiness the other girl carried with her. She would look happy too if Lorimer had given her such a carefully chosen present, had smiled at her so affectionately, had taken her home and shown her how much he loved her.

'Hello, Skye.' Skye could hardly bear the friendliness in Moira's voice. 'I told Lorimer I'd pop in this morning. Is he free?'

'I'm always free for you, Moira, you know that.' Lorimer had appeared in the doorway of his office. His gaze flickered to Skye who was staring at the word-processor screen, unable to watch the happiness in his face as he greeted Moira. 'Come in, Moira...Skye, would you bring us some coffee, please?'

'Of course.' Skye was proud of her cool voice. She pushed back her chair and reached for the tray she always used now to carry the coffee up the stairs from the kitchen. As she stood up, she could hear Lorimer ushering Moira into his office.

'I suppose we'd better put personal feelings aside and discuss how this is going to change things in the future.'

Moira laughed the happy laugh of a woman who knew herself to be loved. 'I don't think it need change things too much. I'd still like to carry on working for you...until we think about having children, of course.'

The door closed behind them. Automatically, Skye went down to the kitchen and poured the coffee. There was only one interpretation she could put on what she had overheard. Lorimer and Moira were going to get married. Why else would Lorimer talk about putting personal feelings aside to discuss business? After all that he had had to say about his disillusion, he was going to marry Moira and take her to live in the manse by the sea and she would be mother to his dark, blue-eyed sons.

What else had she expected?

Skye held herself together by sheer will-power, but she knew that the slightest touch would shatter her into a thousand agonising pieces. She forced herself upstairs and into the office, where Lorimer and Moira were laughing in the intimate way of people who knew each other very well. She set the tray on the desk, placed a cup near Moira, another by Lorimer. She didn't think either of them noticed her go.

Skye sat down at her desk and looked down at her shaking hands. If Lorimer saw her like this, he would have no trouble seeing through her flimsy façade of control to the truth. Somehow she had to convince him that the kisses they had shared, the night she had spent in his arms, the easy friendship they had found walking along the beach...that all these meant no more to her than they did to him.

She felt gripped by a terrible numbness. She knew she should be working, doing something, anything, to take her mind off the thought of Lorimer and Moira together, but she could only stare wretchedly at her screen.

The phone shrilling abruptly beside her made her start violently. Taking several deep breaths, Skye waited until she was composed enough to answer, and then slowly picked up the receiver.

It was Charles, sounding urbane and assured, asking her out to dinner the following evening. He was the last person Skye wanted to see, and she was about to offer an excuse when she heard a burst of laughter from behind the closed door. What better way to convince Lorimer that she wasn't about to sit around pining for him?

'Thank you, Charles,' she said steadily. 'Tomorrow sounds fine.'

CHAPTER TEN

LORIMER was frowning down at the letters she had typed the following afternoon when Charles strolled into the office to pick her up. His expression grew black as he looked from Charles to Skye who had taken extra care with her appearance that day.

'Are you going out?'

'It *is* half-past five,' Skye pointed out sweetly. She had made a great show of greeting Charles, glad that Lorimer was there to notice that she had no eyes for anyone else.

Yesterday's misery had focused into a deep, comforting anger. She was furious with herself for falling in love with Lorimer at all. Why had she let it happen? It wasn't as if he had encouraged her, quite the opposite. He had made a point of telling her how cynical he felt about marriage, so there had been no excuse for her to indulge in any hopes... and then he had turned around and got engaged to Moira! That made Skye even angrier. Why had he bothered to tell her about his parents' separation at all? Whenever she thought about how sympathetic she had been, how understanding, she burned with humiliation. Lorimer hadn't needed her sympathy or her understanding. He had Moira to console him for his past unhappiness. Skye was convinced that he must have guessed how she felt before she did, and had been simply trying to warn her off, and she squirmed at the thought. Had her feelings been that obvious? Were they still?

Her determined display of defiance was all that was keeping Skye going. It was the first day of December. She had three more weeks to get through and keeping her pride was the only way she was going to do it.

So she gave Lorimer the bright smile of a girl without a care in the world and let Charles help her into her coat.

Charles set himself out to be charming. He took Skye to an expensive restaurant and showered her with compliments which left her absolutely cold. She couldn't understand why he was making such a fuss of her. The last time she had seen him, at Fleming's ill-fated dinner party, he hadn't bothered to hide his fastidious dislike of her behaviour, and now here he was, plying her with wine and apparently intent on whispering sweet nothings in her ear.

'I hope we'll be able to see more of each other back in London,' said Charles, refilling her glass.

The thought of London, of anywhere without Lorimer, chilled Skye. 'Are you leaving Edinburgh, then?'

'As soon as I can.' Charles leant forward confidentially. 'The truth is, I'm thinking of moving on, but I need to make sure my reputation precedes me. That means setting up a really profitable deal that'll get my name known in the right circles.'

'I thought you liked working for Fleming?'

Charles shrugged. 'He's a nice chap, but too cautious. He's lost the cutting edge and he knows it. That's one of the reasons he brought me up here, to show the Scottish office how to make a killing.'

It was a horrible term, Skye reflected, unable to believe now that it was the cold, ruthless streak in Charles that she had once found so attractive. He leant forward solicitously and covered her hand with his own.

'You seem different, Skye. Quieter.' He dropped his voice meaningfully. 'More appealing.'

Skye withdrew her hand. She couldn't bear anyone but Lorimer to touch her. 'I'm just a bit tired. I didn't have much of a weekend.'

'I tried to ring you on Saturday but your flatmate told me you were away with Lorimer.' Charles's voice was very casual. 'What have you been up to?'

'We went down to Galloway to look at the site of a new course and hotel...you must know it? It's the one Carmichael and Co are backing.'

'Oh, yes,' said Charles. 'I haven't had much to do with that deal after all. I was to have taken over the negotiations from Fleming, but I got the impression that Lorimer deliberately side-lined me. I was hoping it might lead on to other deals with him—golf is big business nowadays, and he's the man to know. He's staking a lot on this new hotel, but he'd be much better off sticking to where the real money is. I suggested some lucrative projects to him, but he didn't want to know.' He smiled suddenly at Skye and she decided she must have imagined the vengeful look in his eyes. 'Still, it's his loss! If he wants to risk everything for his pet project, that's up to him. Fleming tells me he's got a wonderful site in mind...what's the name of the house again?'

'Glendorie House.'

'Ah, yes, that's it. I gather everything's going ahead as planned?'

Skye nodded. She was glad that he seemed willing to keep the conversation to business. 'It is now. We've got the extra land for the golf course that Fleming was insisting on, and Lorimer's about to close on the deal with the owners of the house. There shouldn't be any more problems. The Buchanans are anxious to sell. They're interested in a smaller house near by and they don't want to lose it. They want to visit their daughter in Australia, too, but they can't afford to go until the sale is completed. I think they feel that if it drags on too long their grandchildren will be grown up before they get there, so they're very keen to get everything tied up.'

'I see.' Charles looked thoughtful, but after a moment he changed the subject to what he would do as soon as he got back to London.

Skye was relieved when the meal was over. Charles had been dropping increasingly suggestive comments as the evening progressed and she longed to be on her own. She tried to call a taxi, but Charles insisted on taking her home in his car and in the end she gave in. The sooner she got back to the flat, the sooner she could shut herself in her room and cry herself to sleep.

She soon wished she hadn't accepted his offer of a lift. Charles kept putting his hand on her thigh no matter how far she edged away and when he stopped the car outside the flat he pounced on her before she had time to get out.

'Come on, Skye,' he sneered when she struggled. 'There's no need to play games any more! Did you think I didn't notice how hard you worked to get my attention in London? You wouldn't have objected then!'

'I've changed,' said Skye frigidly, pushing his hand away.

'Yes, you have, and I like you a lot better this way.' Charles leant closer, his breath hot against her face. 'After all, you deserve some reward for following me all the way up to Edinburgh!' He jerked her face round and kissed her clumsily.

A cold voice at the back of Skye's mind told her that she had asked for this before anger came to her aid and she wrenched herself away. Scrambling out of the car, she slammed the door shut behind her and practically ran across the road to the other pavement where she stopped as suddenly as if she had run into a brick wall.

Lorimer was waiting on the other side, his face twisted with contempt. 'What's the matter? Isn't Charles gentleman enough to see you safely up the dark stairs— or didn't he fall for that line?'

'What are you doing here?' demanded Skye, breathless from the shock of seeing him so unexpectedly.

'My car's parked down here. I was on my way back from visiting friends when I came across that scene of unbridled passion in Charles's car.' The jeering note in his voice cracked her heart and set the seal on her misery. 'You seem to be making some progress with him at last.'

'It must have been all the practice I got in Kielven,' she flashed, furious with him for being so obtuse, furious with herself for still caring so desperately what he thought. This, after all, was what she had wanted him to think, but victory seemed suddenly desolate.

A muscle hammered in Lorimer's cheek. 'I'm glad to know I've been of use,' he said bitterly, and, turning on his heel, he walked off into the night.

There were times that week when Skye wondered if putting herself through the purgatory of every day in the office was worth it. Lorimer only spoke to her when it was absolutely necessary. She knew that it would probably be easier on both of them if she just left, but she couldn't bring herself to say goodbye. In spite of the ghastly atmosphere and the hard, contemptuous look on his face, she still loved him. She still wanted to put her arms around him and breathe in the clean smell of his skin. She wanted to press her lips to his throat and lean into him and hear him say that he would never let her go.

On Friday, Lorimer announced that Angus Buchanan had been on the phone with a minor query and that they had both been invited down to Glendorie for lunch the following Monday. 'I pointed out that there was no need for you to go, but they were very insistent that they wanted to see you so I said I'd take you with me.'

Memories of that last drive over the Devil's Beef Tub were bittersweet for Skye. That trip had brought her both joy and pain, and nothing had been the same since. Now it was bliss to sit in the car mere inches from Lorimer; agony to know that he didn't want her there.

The Buchanans were waiting for them, but whatever their original query had been it had been driven entirely from their heads by a new and much more serious worry.

'We had a visit from a young man called Charles Ferrars on Saturday,' said Angus as soon as they were settled in the sitting-room and the dogs had subsided contentedly at Skye's feet. 'He told us that he represented your investors and that they were withdrawing their backing from you. He didn't say why, only that it wouldn't affect us as they would buy the house directly from us.' Angus looked much older today. 'He offered us a much lower figure than the one we agreed with you, Lorimer, but he said it was the best we'd get. According to him, you wouldn't be in a position to buy anyway once his firm had withdrawn their investment, and he seemed to know all about how anxious we are to move.'

'He also said there was no way a hotel in this area could be profitable,' Isobel Buchanan put in. 'He thought there would be more money in a sort of theme park.' She looked at Lorimer with bewildered eyes. 'We didn't really understand. We thought everything had been agreed. What's going on?'

'I don't know,' said Lorimer, very white about the mouth. 'But I'm going to find out.' He stood up. 'We won't wait for lunch, Isobel. I think I should get back to Edinburgh as soon as possible to sort this out.'

'So you know who this Charles Ferrars is?' said Angus hopefully.

'Oh, yes, I know him.' Skye shivered at the menace in Lorimer's voice. 'And so does Skye.'

He practically dragged Skye outside and shoved her into the car. 'Well?' he demanded furiously as he drove off in a squeal of tyres. 'Would you like to explain what little plan you and Charles have cooked up between you?'

'I don't know anything about it!' said Skye, near to tears.

'Don't come the innocent with me, Skye! You've been very clever at playing the girl who everybody loves, such fun, so pretty, so charming—and so treacherous! Have you had this planned right from the start? Or was giving Charles confidential information the only way you could get him to take any notice of you?'

'No!'

'How did he know to come straight to the Buchanans? Who told him that they were anxious to sell? I didn't tell Fleming that. I'm not reduced to preying on an elderly couple's anxieties yet, but obviously Charles is!'

Skye twisted her hands in her lap, guiltily remembering how she had told Charles all about the Buchanans. 'I told him the deal was going through without problems,' she said in a small voice. 'And, yes, I mentioned that the Buchanans were keen to get everything sorted out, but I didn't know that he was planning this!'

'You might have realised if you'd stopped to think about it, but you didn't, did you?' Lorimer was rigid with fury, his hands gripping the steering-wheel so hard that his knuckles showed white. 'No, all you cared about was the kiss you got as a reward at the end of a profitable evening passing on confidential information!'

'I didn't know it was confidential!' Skye shouted suddenly. 'Charles works for Carmichael and Co. He must have access to all that information anyway.'

'Except that I've been very careful about the information I pass on. I've never trusted Charles Ferrars. I told Fleming I'd only work with him, and I've deliberately kept any information that Charles might get his hands on to a minimum.'

'Why didn't you tell *me* that?' she demanded. She was tired and angry and miserably confused. 'I'm supposed to be your PA. If you hadn't kept me in the dark, I might have known what I could and couldn't say to him.'

'Why should I trust you any more than him?' Lorimer countered scathingly. 'You told me you were in love with him, and I've had more than enough reason to know just how far you're prepared to go to get him.'

Skye slumped back in her seat. 'You've got it all wrong,' she said desperately.

'Oh, I dare say you didn't *mean* to ruin my deal.' Lorimer's contempt was worse than his anger. 'But you've done it anyway. It's always like that with you, isn't it, Skye? You're so spoilt and selfish and superficial, you never give a thought to anybody else caught up in your stupid, childish schemes. You don't care that the Buchanans are sick with worry, that Duncan is going to be disillusioned yet again, that those lovely grounds are going to be ripped up and turned into some plastic theme park. All you care about is Charles!'

Skye turned her head away, too sick at heart to argue. He wasn't going to listen anyway.

They drove all the way back to Edinburgh in glacial silence. Lorimer stopped the car outside her flat. His eyes stared straight ahead over the steering-wheel. 'Get out,' he said with a chilling lack of emotion. 'You've been trouble right from the start. I don't want to hear from you or see you or have anything at all to do with you ever again.'

Skye said nothing. She opened the door and got out, shutting it carefully behind her. Then she stood on the pavement and watched Lorimer drive out of her life while the dammed-up misery burst at last and the tears streamed down her cheeks.

'I'm sure he'll change his mind when he cools down,' said Vanessa several hours later. She had come home from work to find Skye sitting in the middle of the floor with a cold mug of tea beside her and an expression of such despair on her face that Vanessa's heart had failed her. Gradually she had dragged the whole story out of Skye. 'He's just livid about the way that creep Charles has scuppered his deal, but when he's had time to think about it he'll realise how unfair he's been to you. Why don't you go and see him tomorrow and explain exactly what happened?'

'No,' said Skye bleakly. 'I'm not going to try and see him again. I can't bear it. I'm going back to London.'

'It's not like you to give up so easily, Skye. Look what lengths you went to to be near Charles. Surely Lorimer's worth more of an effort than that?'

Skye shook her head. 'It was just a game with Charles. I can't blame Lorimer for not taking me seriously, but what I feel for him is...completely different. I don't want to play games with him. Lorimer deserves better than that. He's said he doesn't want to see me, and I'm not going to inflict myself on him again. In the end, it's going to be easier for both of us if I just go.'

'Oh, Skye!' Vanessa regarded her friend sadly. 'I'll miss you. What are you going to do?'

Distress quivered over Skye's face as she contemplated an empty grey future. 'I don't know.' She took a deep breath and tried to get her wavering voice under control. 'One thing I am going to do is see Fleming and ask him to change his mind about withdrawing his investment. It's all I can do for Lorimer now, and he's too proud to beg himself.'

But when she rang Fleming's office the next day, she was told that he was in London and wouldn't be back until Wednesday. Skye spent the day wandering around Edinburgh. It was very cold and the sky had a leaden look that threatened snow. Christmas lights were strung along the gardens below the castle, soft and blurry in the purplish-blue light, and the Salvation Army band played carols in Princes Street while the crowds of shoppers hurried past. The Christmas cheer only seemed to underline her despair and she turned away from the gay shops to trudge up the Mound towards the castle. The buildings there were tall and grey, although the lights in the windows made beckoning yellow oblongs in the smudgy atmosphere.

Vanessa's prediction that Lorimer would forgive her as soon as he calmed down was proved wrong. An embarrassed Sheila climbed the stairs that evening, having been instructed to rid the office of any trace of Skye. 'What on earth's happened?' she asked, handing over a cosmetic bag, a jumper and two potted plants. 'Lorimer's been in the most filthy mood all day. He won't talk to anyone and he just about bit my head off when I asked where you were. The office isn't the same without you, Skye!'

Skye smiled sadly. 'You'll have to get used to it, I'm afraid.' She hugged Sheila before they both broke down and cried. 'Come and see me if you're ever in London and... and give my love to everybody.'

She rang Fleming first thing the next morning and asked baldly if she could come and see him. 'What's the matter, Skye?' he asked in concern when she arrived. 'I've never seen you in a state like this before.'

Skye hardly heard him. 'I know you've decided to withdraw the finance from Lorimer's project, Fleming,' she launched in at once, 'but won't you please, please reconsider?' Too strung up to sit down, she paced backwards and forwards, twisting her fingers together. 'The project means such a lot to Lorimer, and so many people are going to be disappointed if it doesn't go ahead. The Buchanans, Duncan McPherson, everyone down there who'd like another golf course instead of some theme park they can't use.'

'I think you'd better sit down.' Fleming pushed her firmly into a chair. 'First of all, I haven't withdrawn the finance. Charles mentioned his plan to me on the phone, but it was obvious that his motivation was not so much to increase our profits as to revenge himself on Lorimer for some slight. I gather he refused to work with Charles on some deals he had lined up. Fortunately for Lorimer, I don't care for that way of going about business and Charles and I parted company at the end of last week. I had high hopes of him, because he's a very capable young man, but I'm afraid I'm old-fashioned enough to believe in honouring one's agreements. I don't know whether Charles was just trying to sabotage the project to ruin Lorimer's reputation, or whether he was going to try and raise the finance for his alternative idea elsewhere, but there's never been any question of Carmichael and Co pulling out of the deal we agreed. I told Lorimer that when he rang me in a blazing temper on Monday afternoon. It took a little time for him to calm down and listen to what I had to say, but I managed to get the message through eventually!'

'So he knows?' Skye slumped limply back into her chair and uttered a silent prayer of thanks. 'Then I didn't need to come after all,' she realised after a moment.

'Why *did* you?' Fleming looked at her curiously. 'I wondered if you might be going to plead for me to take Charles back on.'

'You thought I'd come for *Charles*?' Skye stared at him in astonishment.

'It appears I misread the situation,' said Fleming drily. 'I thought you were interested in Charles.'

'I was,' Skye admitted drearily. 'But everything's changed since then.'

Fleming put a comforting hand on her shoulder. 'I think you'd better tell me all about it.'

Skye opened her mouth, closed it, and burst into overwrought tears. Fleming mopped her up patiently and listened as the whole tangled story came out. 'And you haven't told Lorimer that you're in love with him?'

'How can I?' Skye sobbed into a crumpled tissue. 'He's in love with Moira.'

'*Moira*? Are you sure?' She nodded dismally and Fleming frowned. 'I still think you'd be better off telling him how you feel. Or would you like me to tell him for you?'

'No!' Skye sat bolt upright. 'No, Fleming, you must promise me you won't say *anything* to him!'

Fleming sighed. 'If that's the way you want it, but I think you're making a big mistake!'

Everything about the last two months and a half was a mistake, Skye thought as she queued to buy her ticket at Waverley Station. The only way she could make things right was to leave.

Her ticket seemed to burn a hole in her pocket. Unable to face the thought of going back to the flat and packing her suitcase, Skye wandered aimlessly along the streets, up and down narrow steps and through ancient closes. It had snowed last night and the city had a monochrome quality with a thin layer of white spread over the gardens and rooftops and the streets and narrow houses looking blacker than ever in contrast. Skye crossed the High Street and walked up towards The Meadows. People were wrapped in heavy coats, heads down against the stinging flurry of snowflakes that fell every now and then. They looked like dark Lowry figures as they crossed the snow-covered park.

Skye walked more slowly, sniffing the distinctively Edinburgh smell of brewing hops and studying the stark black silhouettes of the trees. She remembered standing at the bus stop looking at the autumn colours and promising herself that by the time the leaves had fallen her life would have changed completely.

Well, it had done. It would never be the same again. Would she have been so excited at the prospect if she had known just how differently she would feel only a matter of weeks later?

Skye was very cold when she finally went back to the flat and there were snowflakes melting on her cheeks and clinging to her lashes. This is the last time I shall climb these stairs, she realised as she trudged upwards, and the thought seemed so unutterably sad that the tears squeezed down her cold cheeks. She had never cried so much before, she thought almost angrily, and brushed at the tears with the back of her hand as she toiled up the last few steps, fumbling in her bag for her key.

Her fingers were numb, and, preoccupied with trying to fit the key in the door, she didn't notice the man standing in the shadow of the stairwell until he spoke quietly.

'Skye?'

Her hand froze at the door and then dropped slowly as she turned. It was Lorimer.

He stepped out of the shadows towards her. 'You've been crying,' he said.

Skye had schooled herself not to torture herself remembering the line of his mouth and cheek, or the way he seemed to represent all that was safe and secure. She had told herself to accept the fact that she would never see him again and now she could only stare at him, drinking in his presence, unable to believe that, after all, he was really there.

She wiped her cheeks automatically. 'I was just sad at the thought of leaving Edinburgh,' she said at last. Her voice was husky with the strain of the last few days.

'You don't have to go.' Lorimer had made no move to touch her. 'I still need a secretary.'

Skye swallowed. 'How long for?'

'Another week. Just until Christmas.'

She hated him then for taunting her like that. At long last an invigorating surge of anger broke through the numb misery that had gripped her since Monday. Did he really expect her to be grateful for the chance of one rotten week working her fingers to the bone for him? And what would happen at the end of it? He wouldn't be able to put her on the train to London fast enough!

'Can't you find anyone else to do your typing and photocopying?' she demanded bitterly. 'You must be desperate if you're reduced to asking me!'

'I am desperate,' said Lorimer. 'I've been desperate ever since I drove off and left you standing on the pavement.' Reaching out, he tucked a curl behind Skye's ear and caressed her cheek very gently. 'If I promise to make it up to you every single day, will you forgive me for the things I said to you that day?'

Her anger evaporated as quickly as it had flared. 'Forgive *you*?' Skye pulled resolutely away from the tantalising, distracting warmth of his fingers. 'I was the one who told Charles about the Buchanans. I didn't mean to be so stupid, but somehow I always seem to end up being that way.' She swallowed. 'I really am sorry.'

'Charles would have found out the information somehow,' said Lorimer gently. 'If I hadn't been so wild with jealousy on Monday, I'd have realised that then.'

Skye stared at him, hardly able to believe what she had heard. 'Jealousy?'

'Didn't you realise?' Lorimer gave a wry smile. 'I've spent the last two months so snarled up with jealousy I could hardly think straight.'

'You mean you were jealous of *Charles*?'

'You told me you were in love with him,' Lorimer reminded her. 'And whenever I thought that I just might be able to persuade you to change your mind, you'd make it very obvious that you were only interested in him.'

'But... but...' Skye was torn between tears and laughter '... I only pretended to be interested in Charles because I thought *you* were in love with Moira.'

'Well, you were wrong,' said Lorimer, taking her hands in his warm clasp. 'I'm in love with quite a different sort of girl.' His voice was very deep as he drew her closer. 'I'm in love with a girl with sunshine in her smile, a girl with the bluest eyes I've ever seen. I'm in love with the funniest, the most infuriating, the most irresistible girl in the world.'

Skye's eyes shimmered with tears and a smile trembled on her lips as a glorious, incredulous happiness seeped through her and dissolved the last shreds of unhappiness. 'Me?' she whispered, and Lorimer smiled a smile that left her weak at the knees.

'You,' he confirmed softly and pulled her into his arms. It was a kiss of indescribable sweetness that went on and on, and they were both so lost in dizzy enchantment that neither of them heard the footsteps coming up the stairs.

'Excuse *me*,' said an arctic voice and Skye jerked away from Lorimer to see Mrs Forsyth regarding them with disfavour. 'You're blocking my way,' she pointed out acidly when they both simply stared at her with dazed expressions.

'Oh, yes, I'm so sorry...' Skye moved hastily aside to let her stalk past.

Mrs Forsyth turned at her door and gave them a quelling look. 'You've got a perfectly good flat to do that sort of thing in.' Her nostrils flared in disgust. 'There's no need for you to be cluttering up the stairs,' she added pointedly and shut the door firmly in their faces.

Skye threw Lorimer a dancing look. 'You've ruined my reputation!'

He grinned. 'In that case, I'll just have to make an honest woman of you! Not that she's not right. We'd be much better off inside. I've been waiting for you on this freezing landing all afternoon and I need to sit down!'

The sitting-room was cluttered with washing and magazines and discarded clothes but Lorimer didn't seem to notice. He sank into one of the armchairs and pulled Skye down on to his lap. 'Where were we before we were so rudely interrupted?'

Skye smiled, put her arms around his neck and reminded him. 'How long had you been waiting?' she murmured against his ear long, breathless minutes later.

'It felt like hours, but it probably wasn't that long. I'd been sitting in my office feeling as if the world had come to an end when Fleming rang. He told me you'd just been round to beg him not to withdraw his investment for my sake and he thought I'd like to know.'

'I particularly asked him not to tell you anything!'

'I'm glad he did. I'd been so convinced that you were in love with Charles, but when I heard that you'd done that for me I began to hope that I might have been wrong after all. So I came straight round here and waited...and waited...and waited! Where *were* you?'

Skye rested her head against his shoulder with a sigh. 'Just wandering around being miserable and imagining how happy you'd be with Moira.'

'What on earth made you think I was in love with *Moira*?'

'She seemed exactly the kind of girl you liked,' she explained. 'And I saw you with her that night when we got back from Kielven. The next day she was wearing that scarf you'd bought her, and she looked so radiant. She was so obviously in love.'

'She is,' Lorimer agreed unexpectedly. 'Very much so, but not with me, you idiot! I took Moira out to dinner to celebrate the fact that she'd just got engaged to Andrew Peters. If you knew anything about golf, you'd know he's Scotland's up-and-coming player. Moira met him when she was organising the Pro-Am competition. Andrew's done very well on the international circuit this year. He's in the States at the moment, which is why I took Moira out on her own. She's one of the nicest people I know, and a good friend. The scarf was an engagement present for her.'

'I wish I'd known,' said Skye. 'She was the only reason I agreed to have dinner with Charles. It was one of the worst evenings of my life! And worst of all was coming face to face with you at the end of it and knowing that you'd seen him kissing me and wouldn't believe that I'd hated every second of it!'

Lorimer's arms tightened around her. 'You thought it was the worst evening of your life, but it was nothing to what I felt! I hadn't been to visit friends at all. I'd finally decided to give in and tell you how I felt about you. I'd tried despising you but it just didn't work. I think I've been in love with you ever since you sat in my office and told me all those absurd stories to try and make me give you the job!

'I didn't want to fall in love with you, Skye. My parents' experience had made me very cynical about marriage, and I'd decided that I wasn't going to risk going through that myself, but meeting you changed everything for me. I discovered that I didn't want a safe, lonely future after all. I wanted you. In spite of everything I thought I knew about marriage, in spite of everything I thought I knew about *you*, you were my one chance of happiness. I didn't know how it had happened, or why, I only knew it was true. It didn't matter how infuriating you were, I couldn't get you out of my mind and that weekend in Kielven only made things worse. Do you know what it was like for me to hold you in my arms all night and know that it left you stone-cold? It took all my self-control to keep my hands off you. I nearly told you on the beach in the dark, but I lost my nerve. Partly pride and partly because I didn't want you to withdraw just when I thought we were becoming friends.

'You didn't make things easy for me, Skye,' he said, taking her hand and pressing a kiss to her palm. 'You felt so right in my arms and looked so right in my house. I only took you there because I wanted to see how the rooms looked with you in them, and I knew then that if you weren't there the house would always seem empty without you, no matter how much furniture I bought. Then I saw you crying and thought you were thinking about Charles.' He paused. 'I was furious with myself for letting myself dream and told myself I'd be far better off if I could just ignore you, but it didn't stop me wanting to thump every man who asked you to dance that evening, and when we danced and I felt you so soft and warm in my hands...well, I lost my head.'

He tilted back Skye's head and smiled ruefully down into her eyes. 'It wasn't fair to kiss you like that, I know, but I had to hold you somehow and if it's any comfort I felt terrible afterwards. That's why I came round that evening, to apologise and to ask if there was any way we could start afresh, but instead I saw Charles kissing you.' He hesitated, then asked abruptly, 'Were you really in love with him, Skye?'

'I thought I was,' she said, 'but it was just a girlish infatuation. I wasn't in love with the real Charles. I think I was in love with the idea of being in love.' She looked deep into Lorimer's eyes, her own blue and warm and shining with happiness. 'That was before I met you and knew what being in love was really like,' she explained and kissed him again. 'Go on,' she said after a while, resting her face against his throat with a contented sigh.

'There isn't much else. I went home thinking what a fool I'd nearly made of myself, and I've been thoroughly unpleasant to you ever since...but it was only because I'm so deeply, desperately in love with you and life just didn't seem worth living without you there to drive me to distraction!'

He held her tightly to him, kissing her until Skye felt as if she was about to dissolve with happiness. 'Are you sure you love me?' she asked, breathless beneath the delicious assault of his hands and the drift of his lips down her throat. 'I'm quite the wrong kind of girl for you.

I'm hopeless and scatty and bad at golf and I'm English and I've got terrible taste in earrings.'

Lorimer raised his head and took her face firmly between his hands. 'I know. Those are severe drawbacks, of course. You're absolutely the last girl I expected to fall in love with, but somehow, in spite of everything, I realised that the wrong girl was the right girl for me after all. The *only* girl.' He smiled lovingly into her eyes. 'And who knows? You might change,' he teased. 'With a little practice, you just might improve at golf, and acquire a taste for pearl studs, but, for the rest, I love you just the way you are.'

'I *could* try and be more efficient and work harder on my typing,' offered Skye, prepared to make any sacrifice to please him.

Lorimer considered. 'I don't think it's worth honing up your secretarial skills just for a week,' he decided. 'After all, Moira will be taking over after Christmas.'

She pulled back and eyed him uneasily, suddenly uncertain. 'You mean you really do only want me for a week?'

'I only need you as a secretary for a week,' said Lorimer. 'After that, I need you as a wife, which calls for quite different skills!'

Mollified, Skye relaxed back against him with a sigh of happiness and kissed his ear. 'How long for?' she whispered, and his arms closed hard around her.

'Forever.'

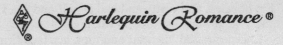

New from Harlequin Romance
a very special six-book series by

The town of Hard Luck, Alaska, needs women!

The O'Halloran brothers, who run a bush-plane service called **Midnight Sons**, are heading a campaign to attract women to Hard Luck. *(Location: north of the Arctic Circle. Population: 150—mostly men!)*

"Debbie Macomber's *Midnight Sons* series is a delightful romantic saga. And each book is a powerful, engaging story in its own right. Unforgettable!"

—Linda Lael Miller

TITLE IN THE MIDNIGHT SONS SERIES:

BRIDE'S BAY RESORT

UNLOCK THE DOOR TO GREAT ROMANCE AT BRIDE'S BAY RESORT

Join Harlequin's new across-the-lines series, set in an exclusive hotel on an island off the coast of South Carolina.

Seven of your favorite authors will bring you exciting stories about fascinating heroes and heroines discovering love at Bride's Bay Resort.

Look for these fabulous stories coming to a store near you beginning in January 1996.

Harlequin American Romance #613 in January
Matchmaking Baby by Cathy Gillen Thacker

Harlequin Presents #1794 in February
Indiscretions by Robyn Donald

Harlequin Intrigue #362 in March
Love and Lies by Dawn Stewardson

Harlequin Romance #3404 in April
Make Believe Engagement by Day Leclaire

Harlequin Temptation #588 in May
Stranger in the Night by Roseanne Williams

Harlequin Superromance #695 in June
Married to a Stranger by Connie Bennett

Harlequin Historicals #324 in July
Dulcie's Gift by Ruth Langan

Visit Bride's Bay Resort each month wherever
Harlequin books are sold.

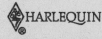

HARLEQUIN ®

BBAYG

Fall in love all over again with

This Time... MARRIAGE

In this collection of original short stories, three brides get a unique chance for a return engagement!

- Being kidnapped from your bridal shower by a one-time love can really put a crimp in your wedding plans! _The Borrowed Bride_— by **Susan Wiggs**, _Romantic Times_ Career Achievement Award-winning author.

- After fifteen years a couple reunites for the sake of their child—this time will it end in marriage? _The Forgotten Bride_—by **Janice Kaiser**.

- It's tough to make a good divorce stick—especially when you're thrown together with your ex in a magazine wedding shoot! _The Bygone Bride_— by **Muriel Jensen**.

Don't miss THIS TIME...MARRIAGE, available in April wherever Harlequin books are sold.

HARLEQUIN ®